HOUSE OF THE FOX

Für Isabelle,
viel Spaß in der Wüste!

Ophelia

HOUSE OF THE FOX

A DESERT MYSTERY

CORNELIA FEYE

KONSTELLATION
PRESS

Published by Konstellation Press, San Diego

Cover design: Scarlet Willette, Max Feye and Sebastian Feye

Editor: Lisa Wolff

ISBN-10: 1480044148

ISBN-13: 9781480044142

For Robert and Dorothy, two wise ones who left us to figure things out on our own

HOUSE OF THE FOX SONG

We are living in the house of the fox
Where time stands still year after year
Where the city is far and the sky is near
Between jagged mountains tinged in red
Sandy plains and pink clouds that bled

The mountain sheep roams shy and rare
Hidden by rocks in the sun's ruthless glare
It crosses the road a moment too late
In the shape of a truck it meets its fate
By a driver speaking on his phone
In a king-size Suburban driving alone

We are living in the house of the fox
Where time stands still year after year
Where the city is far and the sky is near
And the fox disappears in the shadows behind
For a night rendezvous of a special kind

In the desert the fox walks on padded paws
Above soars a falcon with prey in its claws
In search of the well, where the water runs clear
It's all dried up and the fox is near
They cannot escape the fox's house
Where death awaits the desert mouse

CAST OF CHARACTERS

- **Ramon Matus,** Conceptual artist
- **Raoul Matus,** Brother of Ramon, works in family's roofing business
- **Marcos Matus,** Father of Ramon and Raoul, emigrated from Mexico
- **Josefina Matus,** Mother of Ramon and Raoul, wife of Marcos
- **Tina Matus,** Wife of Raoul
- **Jaime Matus,** Son of Raoul and Tina, age fourteen
- **Juan Matus,** Son of Raoul and Tina, age ten
- **Francisco Matus,** Cousin of Raoul and Ramon
- **Diego Matus,** Cousin of Raoul and Ramon
- **Antonio Matus,** Father of Francisco and Diego, brother of Marcos
- **Sandra Matus,** Wife of Antonio, mother of Francisco and Diego
- **Betsy,** Josefina Matus's employer
- **Lizzie Cantor,** Daughter of Ronald Cantor, girlfriend of Ramon Matus
- **Ronald Cantor,** Gallery owner, art dealer of Ramon Matus
- **Lieutenant Thompson,** Deputy sheriff of Borrego Springs
- **Deputy Mai Ling,** Assistant sheriff of Borrego Springs

- **Detective Andy Vincelli,** Chief inspector at San Diego Police Department
- **Detective Henderson,** San Diego Police, assistant to Vincelli
- **Lieutenant Brian McInness,** Border patrol officer
- **Jerome Schlesinger,** Self-help guru and author
- **Hilde Schlesinger,** Wife and business manager of Jerome Schlesinger
- **Vega Stern,** Art historian
- **Greg Stern,** Vega's husband
- **Stevie Stern,** Son of Vega and Greg, age nine
- **Daniel Stern,** Son of Vega and Greg, age fourteen
- **Bertrand,** Restaurant owner, Borrego Springs
- **Bill,** Owner of the Desert Rose Café
- **Paula Patterson,** Journalist
- **Mrs. Shmelkes,** Neighbor of Lizzie Cantor

1

THURSDAY, DECEMBER 19, 5:30 A.M.

His day began before dawn. The air was so cold that he could see the breath coming like steam from his nostrils. To keep warm, he broke into a light trot following a track into the deep desert. The frosty morning air had not produced any moisture or dew on the sparse shrubs and wrinkled cacti. The ocotillo and teddy-bear cholla looked as beige and dry as the sandy ground. The air was still; not the slightest breeze stirred the leaves. No birdcall broke the silence. As he trotted through this silent world, he suddenly realized that he was not alone. He detected a human presence close by. Motionless, he sniffed the air for any smell other than desert sage and mesquite bark. From the direction of the canyon came a faint and unfamiliar scent and a subdued flutter of movement. It was too early for the hawks to fly in search of prey, but he realized that dark birds circled the updrafts ahead of him. They were not hawks, however. They were turkey vultures. He followed their trail and came to the edge of the Canyon-Without-Name. Below he saw a scene of frantic activity. Vultures had landed on a body lying on his back in the sand. They picked at his eyes and hands. Some of them hopped away with morsels of flesh; others competed for space on the corpse's face. Just then the first fiery sun rays broke free from the mountain's edge. The sky immediately lit up in orange and yellow streaks of light. The range loomed as a black silhouette before the rising sun, unable to hold back the light and the new day any longer. The desert fox trotted down into the canyon to join the feast.

THURSDAY, DECEMBER 19, 9:00 A.M.

Carefully putting one foot in front of the other, Stevie negotiated the narrow ridge of the desert path leading up to the wind caves. He had left his parents far behind. His mother, Vega, knew he wanted to make sure she was out of sight before he started skipping over the small boulders on the trail. It was the only way to avoid her shouting anxious warnings each time his sneakers caused a cascade of loose pebbles to descend into the adjoining canyon. Nine-year-old Stevie as well as his fourteen-year-old brother, Daniel, could handle this trail. They were getting used to being out in the open desert, where they could see for miles without a man-made structure obstructing their view. No power lines, no roads, just layers of rock in hues from rose to ocher to chalk white.

"Look at me, Dad," Stevie called back to his father, "I'm Frodo, the hobbit, following Gandalf on the way to Mordor!"

"You are about the right size, too," his father, Greg, called back.

"I just hope you don't bring the night riders down on us!" shouted Vega.

"Mom, death and evil are everywhere; you can't escape them."

"We can try. At least watch out for rattlesnakes and tarantulas."

"Mom, don't worry so much. We are fine."

~

Daniel had already reached the wind caves. He sat in one of them, waving. Oval caverns carved out by wind and weather in the soft sandstone, the wind caves were stacked like apartments on top of each other. They provided views over miles of desert to the mountains in the far distance. The boys loved to climb in them. Vega loved to sit in them and look out into the distance, letting her thoughts go as far as they wanted, without any distractions or walls to limit them. There was no movement except for the faint rustling in an ocotillo bush, some birds circling overhead. She could hear the whistling of the wind in the cavities of the caves, and the shouts of the boys as they discovered yet another crevice to explore. Otherwise the desert was completely silent. So silent, it almost hurt her ears. The absence of all the customary background noise like cars in the distance, a telephone ringing, a radio, a plane flying over, a neighbor's TV set, or the humming of a refrigerator was almost unsettling.

As Vega contemplated the emptiness of the desert and the silence around her, it was shattered by a piercing scream.

Vega and Greg rushed to the spot where Stevie stood screaming at the edge of a steep canyon. He pointed down to the bottom of the valley, thirty meters below.

"What is it, Stevie?" Vega tried to calm him.

"The leg and the birds . . ." he gasped.

Below them, in the northern reaches of the Canyon Sin Nombre, a flock of turkey vultures had descended into a tight cluster. They fought for space on their prey, from which only a bloody leg emerged.

Greg clapped his hands and shouted as he ran down into the arroyo, chasing the vultures away. They reluctantly revealed the body of a man, or what was left of him. Splayed at an impossible angle, his eyes picked out by the vultures.

Vega took Stevie into her arms and covered his eyes to keep him from seeing more than he already had. Greg tried to call 911 from his cell phone.

"I can't get any reception!" he called to Vega.

"We are too remote!" she called back.

Daniel gazed at the canyon in shock, his hands covering his mouth, trying to stifle a scream. Vega walked over and put an arm around him.

"What are we going to do?" he asked with a shaky voice. "We can't just leave him here."

"We'll have to. He is beyond help," said Greg, and he took a picture of the corpse. He climbed out of the canyon to the top of the caves, trying to make his call, but without success.

"We'll drive out and report the body," declared Greg calmly, and he began to walk toward their car. The boys scrambled after their father. Nobody spoke a word on their hike back. Their Toyota 4Runner was the only car at the sand-covered parking place for the wind caves. Its tires kicked up small dust devils as they made a hurried exit.

"What happened to that man?" Stevie finally asked.

"He probably fell down the canyon," said Greg.

"Dad, he did not just hurt himself, he was dead! I saw the birds pecking at his eyes," insisted Stevie.

"If you know everything, why do you ask?" said Daniel angrily.

They had reached Split Mountain, where the rough dirt road ran along the side of a steep cliff face, stretching up four hundred feet into the sky. Layers of rock sediment displayed the geological history of the Anza-Borrego Desert's last two million years. Pink, white, yellow, and beige stripes of stone formations piled on top of each other. The pitted "road" was actually a dry riverbed. As Greg navigated the deep ruts, Vega and the boys bumped up and down on their seats.

Coming out of the shadow of the cliff after a bend in the road, they encountered a group of five men walking along the path. They wore tattered jeans, thin-soled tennis shoes, and faded baseball caps, and each carried a small backpack.

"Mexican migrants," said Vega.

"What are they doing here, Mom? It's so far from everything!" Stevie demanded to know.

"Yes, they are very far from home," Vega admitted.

"Actually, we're not that far from the Mexican border," said Daniel. "It runs just a few miles south of here."

"But where are they going? And where did they stay overnight? It will take them too long to get to the Casa," Stevie wondered.

"I don't think they're going to the Casa, Stevie," said Greg.

La Casa Del Zorro was the luxurious but struggling desert resort where the Stern family stayed during their excursion into the Anza-Borrego Desert.

"Are you stupid, Stevie?" Daniel accused his brother. "Don't you see they're illegal Mexicans? They have no money, and they don't even have a sleeping bag."

"That's what I'm worried about," said Vega as they passed the group slowly. The men stopped and looked at the family inside the car with dark, fearful, and suspicious eyes.

"Are we just going to leave them here?" asked Stevie, incredulous.

"Yes, Stevie, we have a dead body to report," Greg said firmly.

3

THURSDAY, DECEMBER 19, 10:00 A.M.

The Desert Rose Café sat next to the Anza-Borrego airstrip, right across from the off-road vehicle terrain. To its owner, Bill, it was the perfect location. Dirt bikes and dune buggies cut deep tire tracks into the sandy ground; the roars of their engines pierced the silence of the surrounding desert park. Scattered houses laid claim to plots of dry land, and tattered tin mailboxes along the S1 road hinted at dwellings in this enclave inside the state park. Here the dirt bikes ruled. Dust swirled behind the racing vehicles and few cacti stood a chance of survival in their path.

The Desert Rose Café did not keep the promise its name implied. There were no roses anywhere. It wasn't much of a café, either. Just a trailer overlooking a dusty parking lot, where the off-road vehicles congregated before attacking the desert dunes.

Bill looked out through the grimy window onto this lot and watched his friend Bob dismount from a dirt bike. Bob had just torn up the racecourse in record time. Bill had heard his engine whine as Bob pushed it to its limits. It was a slow day, and Bill looked forward to a leisurely chat with Bob about his ride.

A burly man with a bushy mustache, a braided ponytail, and a Guns N' Roses tattoo on his considerable shoulder, Bill enjoyed showing off his muscles underneath his black sleeveless T-shirt. He ran the Desert Rose Café not because he had any particular culinary skills, but because he liked dirt bike racing and he could not live in the city. Not anymore. It was too confining. He had done the city life for too long: being part of a motorcycle gang, working in a garage, drinking, driving, doing the odd burglary jobs, and living in a miserable rented room.

He had done some time in jail, and when he came out to the desert after his release he just stayed, lived in a trailer, worked in a trailer. He had a view and space around him. He had even given up drinking. Almost. Mostly he drank coffee, black and a bit burned from standing on the coffee machine for too long. Just like now. He took a sip and considered making a fresh pot, but he was in no hurry. Customers were not exactly rushing in the door. Bob only drank beer anyway.

Bill blinked as he saw a white SUV drive onto the dirt lot in front, coming to a screeching halt. Probably some hiker who had gotten lost and needed directions. Nature lovers did not usually frequent his business. They wanted salads or vegetables or whatever it was they ate. The Desert Rose's menu offered burgers, hot dogs, chips, coffee, ice cream and beer. As far as Bill was concerned, that was all anyone needed.

A family of four, including a light-haired young boy and a teenager, scrambled up the stairs into his trailer. Bill regarded them thoughtfully. They looked frazzled. They must be really lost.

"I need to make an urgent phone call!" declared the man after entering the dining room. He was tall with dark curly hair and looked like he was used to being in charge.

"Nothing's that urgent around here," replied Bill.

"This is," countered the man. "We just found a dead man in the Canyon Sin Nombre by the wind caves."

"O jeez, another one bit the dust. They just keep coming. Don't have enough water. Don't know the way. They fall or freeze or die of dehydration." Bill sighed. "Cell phone didn't work? You can use my phone."

The small boy looked up at Bill with huge eyes.

"What's up, little man? Had a bit of a shock, haven't you? How about a milk shake for you and your brother?"

The boys nodded, relieved, eying Bill's spiked bracelets and skull belt buckle.

"Thank you, that's very kind," said the woman, a slim blonde with short hair and a T-shirt displaying some kind of Indian design. Bill turned to his blender and started to throw bananas, ice cream, and milk into it.

"I'm Bill," he said over his shoulder.

"I'm Stevie, and this is my brother, Daniel." Stevie extended a small hand.

"I'm the owner of the Desert Rose." Bill turned around and shook it.

"It's very nice," was the woman's lame comment.

"It's a bit off the beaten track, but I like it. We have one of the best off-road sites in Southern California. People come from LA, Bakersfield, San Diego, from all over really." He ran the blender, then poured the shakes into glasses for the boys.

"Those bikes are cool," said Stevie, pointing out the window at the parking lot."You like them? The black one with the red and orange fire design is mine. It won the Baja 1000 race three times in a row."

"Wow, how fast can it go?" asked Daniel, sucking on the straw of his milk shake.

Before Bill could answer, Daniel's father interrupted, turning back from the telephone:

"Okay, Sheriff Thompson of Borrego Springs is meeting me here as soon as he can make it. I'll go back to the site with him. You guys don't have to wait here. Why don't you take the car and go back to the Casa?"

"Can we just finish our milk shake?" asked Stevie.

"Sure. What do I owe you?" The man turned to Bill.

"Nothing—this one's on the house. Sheriff Thompson will take care of the body. It happens around here. He knows what to do."

"How unfortunate that this kind of thing happens regularly. We just saw a group of five migrants walking in the canyon leading to the wind caves," the woman said.

"Well, they think they can just walk through the desert like it's a Sunday stroll. Their 'coyotes' take their money and give them the wrong information. They leave them on their own without enough water. If they make it to the Desert Rose, I give them water and send them on their way, but I don't know where they end up. Poor devils. Why don't they just stay where they are?"

"Maybe they don't have a choice," the woman said, but Bill just stared her down.

Outside, the red and blue flashing lights of Sheriff Thompson's police cruiser announced the arrival of the law. No sirens were necessary on the empty roads. Before the father of the family had time to go out and meet him, the sheriff entered the trailer and seemed to fill it up completely. His tall and bulky frame took up all the space in the doorframe. He tipped his hat to Bill, and Bill answered with a short "Sheriff."

"Well, so what have we got here?" he boomed at the family. Next to Sheriff Thompson they looked diminutive.

"I'll see you back at the hotel," the woman said to her husband as she gathered up the boys.

"Can I go with Daddy in the police car, please?" Stevie pleaded, looking with awe at the flashing lights as they walked out.

4

THURSDAY, DECEMBER 19, 10:00 A.M.

At the end of Interstate 8, as far west from Borrego as a car could drive, on the lush coastal peninsula of Point Loma, Betsy placed a twig of blooming purple bougainvillea on the silver tray. She had lined it with two snow-white overlapping linen napkins and placed a carefully chosen blue bowl with fresh strawberries on them. On a small plate next to the bowl was a cheese sandwich with a slice of cucumber. A glass of orange juice in a crystal tumbler and a mini bag of potato chips completed the arrangement. Betsy smiled as she moved the bag of chips to the rim of the tray. Normally she would never include such a lowbrow food item. She prided herself on providing only the best quality foods to her family and friends, but this tray was for Josefina, Betsy's cleaning lady. Josefina was from Mexico and came every other Thursday. In sketchy English, Josefina had thanked Betsy for her previous lunches and told her that the chips were her favorite.

Even though Josefina had broken four valuable English crystal tumblers, Betsy still regarded her as part of the family. Betsy's family was very small, just she and her husband. No kids, and her relatives were all back in England. So she'd adopted Josefina. She liked to feed people; it made her feel abundant and generous. Betsy knew she didn't look like the food lover she was. She was proud of her petite, slim figure and wore clothes size 1. Seventy years of life had not hampered her energy and appetite for life. Betsy felt blessed, and rightfully so. She loved her husband and had a beautiful home close to the beach and a closet full of adorable outfits, which she chose with as much care as her food.

"Darling, you are up already?" Betsy saw her husband coming into the kitchen.

"Is this my breakfast?" he asked sleepily.

"No, darling, yours is on the dining room table. I would never give you potato chips for breakfast, you know that. This tray is for Josefina. She is coming today."

Betsy's husband grumbled something and moved out to the dining area.

"Bye, darling. Have a lovely day, darling!" she sang as she moved out the door. "Be nice to Josefina if you see her."

"I thought she was our cleaning lady, and a pretty clumsy one at that, not the guest of honor," her husband replied.

But Josefina never came that day. The bougainvillea twig wilted and the bag of potato chips remained unopened.

THURSDAY, DECEMBER 19, 11:00 A.M.

Fifteen miles south and a whole world away, Josefina, Marcos's wife for forty-four years, sat on her side of the bed they shared. They lived in Barrio Logan, a San Diego neighborhood close to the Mexican border, in a small three-bedroom house they shared with their son Raoul, his wife, Tina, and their two grandsons, Jaime and Juan. Marcos put his arm around Josefina's shaking shoulders. She sobbed and her tears soaked the lime-green bedspread with the yellow ruffles. Few rays of sunlight made it into the bedroom through the narrow window, which Josefina had decorated with a home-sewn lace curtain.

Marcos stroked her red hair, held in an unruly bun. He noticed the gray roots, her wrinkled face, and her figure, which had gone out of shape, but he still loved his wife tenderly. His own eyes were wet, but he did not cry. He had to be strong. Since his early days as an illegal immigrant farmworker, sleeping in barns or sheds so he could send his money home to Mexico, he had been through too much to break down now.

Marcos came from Sonora, where his Yaqui Indian tribe had been persecuted since the early 1800s. By coming to America he had not only escaped the grinding poverty, but also oppression by Mexican authorities. After years of farmwork, Josefina finally joined him north of the border. Their two sons, Raoul and Ramon, were born here and had American citizenship. Their family had been lucky, until now. Now only one of their children was left. Their older son was dead.

"We have to go and bring him home!" sobbed Josefina.

Marcos nodded. "We will."

"Why was he out in the desert?!"

"I don't know."

"What did the sheriff say?"

"He said they found him in the Canyon Sin Nombre."

"How can the canyon have no name?"

"Canyon Sin Nombre *is* the name."

"Ramon had no reason to be in the desert. He has an apartment in town."

"We'll find out if he left a message," Marcos assured her.

"What message? Why didn't he call us, if he had a message?"

"They need to find out why he was in the desert."

"Who is 'they'?"

"The sheriff and the police."

"What do they care? He is dead."

"It is their job."

"What does his brother say?"

"Raoul will come with us to Borrego Springs."

"We worked so hard to get out of the desert!"

"We did, *mi amor.*"

"Ramon was doing so well. I was proud of him."

"Something must have happened."

"What happened? What went wrong?"

"That's what they have to find out."

Josefina put her head on Marcos's shoulder and closed her eyes. Apparently she had run out of questions for now. She would let him decide what to do next.

THURSDAY, DECEMBER 19, 11:00 A.M.

Deputy Sheriff Thompson had a dilemma. He had a dead Mexican on his hands, which was not in itself unusual. It happened periodically, normally in the summer when the heat rose to 115 degrees. It was rarer in the middle of winter, when the temperature stayed a pleasant 75 degrees like today. Of course, some Mexicans died of exposure in the winter, because they did not realize how cold it could get at night. But the Mexican in the morgue at the Borrego Medical Clinic was not the usual illegal border crosser dying of lack of water or exhaustion. This one wore stylish leather loafers, not thin-soled tennis shoes. He had an American driver's license with a San Diego address in his pocket.

The sheriff's deputy, Mai Ling, had immediately located and notified his relatives. The parents and brother were on their way to identify the body. Thompson did not look forward to this encounter. It was always heart-wrenching to meet grieving relatives, but in this case it was even worse. First of all, there was basically no face left. Second, he had no explanation for how this death had occurred.

Things like this were not supposed to happen in Borrego Springs. The last fatality, besides the illegal immigrants, which the Border Patrol took care of, had been the editor of the local bimonthly newspaper, *The*

Borrego Sun, who was killed by her husband, who then shot himself, in 2011. Since then, his job had mainly consisted of locking up the occasional drunk until he sobered up enough to go home.

Sheriff Thompson liked it that way. He had put on some weight in the last couple of years and he did not need the excitement. It was bad for his blood pressure. He would let his deputy deal with the relatives. They probably did not speak any English anyway. Despite the fact that Mai Ling was of Korean origin (or was it Vietnamese? he couldn't quite remember), she spoke Spanish fluently. Besides Korean or Vietnamese or whatever. Not that it did any good here. No Asian people came to Borrego Springs, not even as tourists. She had nobody to converse with in her native language.

Thompson somehow resented Ling's language skills. She was efficient and knew how to handle the computer expertly. She filled out the paperwork for the county office so perfectly, it was outright maddening. She was punctual and friendly on top of it, so it was hard to get mad at her. But he had intuition on his side. Ling was never going to be able to match that. Plus, he could deal with the Border Patrol officers, big guys like his friend McInness, while Ling got flustered in their presence.

That reminded him he had to call McInness. He picked up the phone on his battered wooden desk and looked through the glass doors into the parking lot of the small shopping mall where his office was located.

Outside, Ling greeted an elderly Mexican couple and a younger man with long black hair in a ponytail. They had to be the parents and the brother of the victim. He supposed he had to say hello and express his condolences, but then he was going to send them on their way to the hospital.

He'd pop over to see his friend Bill and have a beer at the Desert Rose later. Chatting with Bill usually triggered his ideas, and he would have to come up with some really good ideas to solve this murder case.

THURSDAY, DECEMBER 19, 11:05 A.M.

"Thank you for coming to Borrego Springs." Deputy Ling extended her hand and Josefina shook it. She was surprised to be greeted by this slim, young Asian woman in a blue uniform. Where was the sheriff?

"My name is Mai Ling, and I am the sheriff's deputy. I'll accompany you to the medical center, where the body is currently held, so you can identify him."

"Where is the sheriff?" asked Marcos.

"He is right here in his office. He's handling the communication with the Border Patrol and the San Diego Police Department, since the victim carried a driver's license with a San Diego address. There is a lot of paperwork and coordination to be done," explained Ling.

Just then Sheriff Thompson came down the steps from his office and approached them.

"Thanks for coming out here, folks. You are in good hands with Deputy Ling here. She'll take good care of you. The most important thing for you is to identify the victim." He held out a huge hand, which Marcos took but Josefina shrank away from.

"I want to see where he was found," requested the younger man, who introduced himself as Raoul, the victim's brother.

"Well, folks, that's a bit out of the way. He was found in the Canyon-Without-Name, out by the wind caves. A forensic team has been going over the site."

"I would like to see it," Raoul insisted calmly.

"If you want to spend one hour driving out through Split Mountain and hike into the canyon for another hour, you are welcome to do so."

"I do, Sheriff. I would like to see where my brother died."

"We don't know if he died there; that's just where he was found. And you first have to identify the body," corrected Thompson.

"I'll go with them, Sir," offered Ling.

"Go ahead then. I have paperwork to do." He nodded curtly to the group and returned to his office.

THURSDAY, DECEMBER 19, 12:30 A.M.

In Mai Ling's police jeep, Josefina, Marcos, and Raoul bumped along the deep ruts of Split Mountain Road. Josefina still felt chills from their visit at the morgue. Marcos and Raoul had identified the body, while she waited in the drab corridor of the Health Center's basement where it was cold and dim. When they emerged again from the room, both her husband and son had looked ashen. They just nodded to her. Marcos took her by the arm and led her back to the jeep with a hard grip.

Now she stared in awe at the sheer cliffs rising on both sides in multicolored layers of rock formations. She had never seen so many shades of tan, beige, red, and yellow sandstone, like the layer cake she sometimes baked.

"Seven million years ago the Gulf of California extended inland into the Anza-Borrego desert. Scattered along the wash, fossilized remains of oysters and pecten shells are embedded in the butte, which used to be part of the ocean," Ling explained.

"We'll drive to the end of Split Mountain and for a short while on Fish Creek Wash until Mud Hills Wash. Then we will have to hike up to the wind caves and the Canyon Sin Nombre. Have you ever been here?"

"No, never," Josefina admitted. "How do you know your way around here so well?"

"It's part of my job. I explore a different corner of the desert every week. I actually have come to enjoy it, especially now in the winter. It can get hellish in the summertime."

"I've been here before, with my brother," Raoul said quietly. "He did some work in the Carrizo Badlands and the Jacumba Mountains."

"So he was here before?" Ling asked quickly.

"Yes, he knew the area. He wouldn't have done anything foolish to endanger himself."

"What kind of work did he do here?"

"He did a land art project. He wrapped rocks in red ribbons like presents and placed them as directional markers along the washes to guide the migrants to safety."

"I didn't know about that project!" exclaimed Josefina.

"He did it last spring after five migrants died of exposure. I came with him and helped him distribute the rocks and take photographs to document the project."

"Your brother was an activist?" asked Ling.

"He was a conceptual artist," said Raoul.

They had reached the hard-packed sandy parking area.

"It's a bit of a climb," warned Ling. "Are you up for it?" she asked Josefina.

"I am strong. I will go with you." Josefina worked hard every day cleaning rich people's houses. She climbed ladders to dust shelves and wash windows. She bent over to clean bathtubs and toilets. She carried heavy water buckets to wash floors. A little climb was not going to keep her away from her older son's last place on earth.

Slowly they made their way up the narrow path and into the Canyon Sin Nombre. A square area was roped off with yellow crime scene tape. It looked like the frame of an artwork. A picture of sand, pebbles, and some small lichen, exactly like rest of the canyon floor, except that it was framed and therefore more important.

There was no blood or indentation from her son's body, Josefina noticed. The wind had taken care of that. The blood had disappeared into the sand. The desert had recreated a clean slate, as it always does.

Humans have tried to change the desert and make it more livable, Josefina thought. *Eventually they give up and the desert returns to its original state.*

"How did he die?" Raoul asked.

"Apparent head injury. The autopsy will tell us more," answered Ling.

"It was an accident?" Raoul asked.

"The head trauma may have been inflicted," Ling said evasively.

Josefina made the sign of the cross in front of the square and said a Hail Mary, quickly and quietly. Marcos stood by her side with his baseball hat in his hands. Raoul prowled the area.

"What are you looking for, Raoul?" Josefina asked.

"I don't know what I'm looking for; a clue, a trace of Ramon," he said.

But there was just the whistling of the wind in the caves above and the great silence of the desert, swallowing their grief.

THURSDAY, DECEMBER 19, 5:00 P.M.

After reading May Ling's accurately and neatly typed report on the site visit and the victim's identification by the Matus family, Sheriff Thompson took off his reading glasses and rubbed the bridge of his nose. He decided to drive over to the Desert Rose Café for a bite to eat.

"Bill, I am at my wits' end about this murder," he complained while trying to get comfortable on the wooden stool at the counter of the Desert Rose.

Bill thoughtfully took a sip of burned coffee.

"I don't know what to tell ya," he said. "Coulda been the drug cartel scum, that's my guess."

"I just don't know what a conceptual artist had to do with the drug cartel. You ever even heard that word 'conceptual artist'?"

"Can't say I have," admitted Bill. "He might've just been in the wrong place at the wrong time."

"He chose an awfully out-of-the-way wrong place to be at the wrong time," considered Thompson after a deliberate sip of beer.

"How about a hot dog? It's almost dinnertime," offered Bill. Thompson was the only customers in the trailer.

"Sure. I always think better with food in my belly," Thompson agreed.

"What's that mean anyway, 'conceptual artist'?" wondered Bill.

"It means he worked with ideas. I had to Google it on my computer."

"Can you make money working with ideas?" Bill was dumb-founded.

"Apparently. He had nice leather loafers on and an expensive gold watch. Supposedly he was almost famous."

Bill whistled as he fired up his hot plate and pulled a package of Oscar Mayer sausages from the fridge.

"He musta had some awfully good ideas."

Sheriff Thompson pondered that statement for a moment.

"I don't know, Bill. He did get himself killed, remember?"

"True. His ideas didn't do him any good in the end, I suppose."

"I still don't understand why someone would want to kill an artist like that. It sounds like he was harmless enough."

Bill slapped the sausages onto the hot plate and put four bun halves into his oversized toaster. He placed the yellow mustard and the red ketchup plastic bottles in front of the sheriff.

"Condiments? Pickles? Onions? Sauerkraut?" Bill was all business.

"Sure, I'll have all the trimmings."

Bill finished preparing the hot dogs and served them in rectangular cardboard trays. The sheriff took a big bite and chewed thoughtfully.

"He must've made some enemies," Bill finally said. "I heard some-where that most murders are committed because of money, or love gone wrong, or both."

"That's a good point, Bill. I'll have to find out about the women in the dead artist's life."

FRIDAY, DECEMBER 20, 3:00 A.M.

Wide awake, Tina lay in the bed she shared with her husband, Raoul, in the house she shared with her in-laws, Josefina and Marcos. She saw the faintly glowing numbers on the alarm clock next to her bed: 3:00 a.m., the witching hour. She often woke up at this time of the morning. Quietly, Tina adjusted her position in bed so as not to wake Raoul. His breathing was slow and regular. Tina tried to breathe deeply and slowly as well, but she knew she would lie here for hours, trying to rein in her thoughts and worries. Her legs itched and she felt hot. Should she get up and open the window wider? Or would that only wake her up even more?

She thought about her shopping list on the refrigerator. She must remember to buy laundry detergent tomorrow, milk and tuna fish. They'd also run out of paper towels and she hadn't added them to her list. Hopefully she wouldn't forget once she was at the store. She turned to the other side. How ridiculous to worry about your shopping list at three in the morning! Everything seemed much bigger and much more important at night. Paper towels really weren't very important.

Josefina was important, and Tina's teenage son, Jaime. Where was he, anyway? Had he come back and snuck in? She didn't think so. Like many mothers, she had a sixth sense for her son and usually woke up when he came home. She was worried about Jaime. He had changed from the sweet boy he used to be. Tina felt she couldn't reach him anymore, even when he sat at the dinner table. He was in his own world and he had no intention of sharing his thoughts with her. Images of a smiling Jaime running along the beach with his kite emerged in her mind. Those days were over. She had to learn to let go and not treat him like a little boy anymore, even if it hurt. Now she had to try to develop a different relationship with this new Jaime; somehow she had to get to know him all over. Except that he didn't seem very interested in a relationship with her.

And what about Raoul? What about their relationship? Tina wasn't sure how well it was going. She didn't want to think about that right now, because that would surely keep her awake. She wanted to think of something soothing, something calm; she really needed peace. There was enough conflict in her life. What could she think about that was relaxing and calm? A sunny day at the beach; a slight breeze; the salty smell in the air; faint voices of children playing, running back and forth; feeling the contours of her body mold the warm sand around her... She also had to pay the electricity bill tomorrow; it was the last day, or else the company could shut off their lights.

Why couldn't she shut off the voice in her head and just go to sleep? Why did it keep hammering on and on? She needed her sleep; there was so much she had to face in the morning. If she was exhausted, how could she cope? Maybe she should take a sleeping pill. There was still a bottle of them in her bathroom cabinet. Tina glanced at the clock again: almost 4:00. It was too late to take a pill. By the time it took effect, it would be almost 5:00, and she had to get up at 6:00 to make breakfast for Raoul and his father, Marcos, before they went to work.

But what could she do for Josefina? Tina had always gotten along well with her mother-in-law. Josefina worked; she also helped in the house and the kitchen. When the boys were small, Josefina had watched her grandsons when she needed help. Now Josefina needed help. What could Tina do for her? What could anybody do for a mother who'd lost her son? Tina shuddered at the thought of losing one of her children. *I wouldn't survive*, she thought; *I would go mad.*

That was probably happening to her mother-in-law right now. Josefina was quietly going mad. Surely she was lying awake as well. Tina wanted to help Josefina, but how could anyone comfort a grieving mother? She could make her favorite food, but Josefina was not eating. The only one who could comfort her now was Raoul.

Tina turned around to her husband's broad back beside her. She noticed his cell phone on the nightstand blinking and vibrating. He picked it up and texted a message.

"Who are you texting?" she asked.

"Nobody. Go back to sleep."

"I can't sleep. Talk to me."

"It was Lizzie. I have to call her back. She doesn't know about Ramon yet."

"What was Ramon doing in the desert?"

"Tina, I don't know. Some art project."

"I always thought Ramon was a real survivor."

"He wasn't. Now go back to sleep."

"Don't talk to me like that. I'm not a child. Why do you have to talk to Lizzie at four thirty? Can't this wait until morning?"

"Tina, be reasonable. She lost her boyfriend. Someone has to tell her."

"Why you?"

"Who else? I don't want to have this conversation right now."

He got up and went out. Tina heard his low voice on the porch below.

11

FRIDAY, DECEMBER 20, 4:30 A.M.

L izzie woke up with a gasp. The green numbers on the alarm clock informed her that it was four thirty. A scrap of a dream floated just barely out of reach of her consciousness. She tried to grasp it, but it was too late; it had already dissolved into the gray predawn. What had woken her up and left small, sweaty beads of fear on her upper lip?

Ramon shot into her mind. She hadn't heard from him all week. He was probably off doing one of his projects, but usually he sent her at least a text message, or an image with a detail of his installations. Not this time. He hadn't answered her texts or calls. She was used to him going off on his own. But normally he kept her up to date on what he was doing. After all, she wasn't just his girlfriend; she was also the daughter of the gallery owner who represented his work. Without his gallery, he was nothing; his projects were just castles in the sand nobody knew about.

Someone had to document his work to make it count, to make it real. Was it enough for him to do these land art projects in the desert if nobody saw them? Would anybody care? He needed someone to tell people about his art, exhibit it, show photographs of it, share the experience, or else why be an artist at all? He needed the gallery to give validation to his work. And that's where she came in. That was her role in their partnership.

Lizzie's mind was racing now. She thought about Ramon with his olive skin and his sharp, Indian features; his long black hair that he sometimes wore in a ponytail, sometimes loose. She thought about his mischievous eyes and his charisma. He could declare anything art and people would believe him and love it. Like the cheap, used tennis shoes he had spray-painted gold and put on a pedestal in the gallery next to the silver ones with little wings attached. Lizzie pictured his work: strange, dreamlike installations of sand, flowers, and darkness.

They had met at an art opening. Lizzie thought they made such a pretty pair. Her blond hair, golden skin, and blue eyes contrasted perfectly with his darkness and intensity. Initially she was sure that was also the attraction for him. He was flattered by her attention. Lizzie was the daughter of one of the most important gallery owners in Los Angeles. She was pretty and she wasn't stupid. Ramon knew she was good for his image. They started going to gallery openings together. Mostly they moved in Lizzie's world of museums, galleries, and clubs. He never took her on his trips into the wilderness or the desert. That made him even more irresistible to Lizzie. She wanted to penetrate that magical world of his, that place from which he drew his inspiration. Even though she hadn't quite succeeded yet, she had made some progress. He sent her pictures from the "other side," which sometimes meant the other side of the border and sometimes the other side of his personality, the one he didn't show in public.

Lizzie noticed her cell phone glowing in the dark. Maybe a picture had arrived while she slept. She grabbed the phone, but it was just a text message from Ramon's brother, Raoul.

"Call me about Ramon," was all it said. She texted back immediately, but didn't expect an answer at this hour: "Where is he?" The reply came right away. Apparently Raoul was awake as well.

"Ramon is gone."

To hell with his sleeping wife beside him and his children and parents in the next room. Lizzie pushed the call button. "What do you mean, 'gone'?" she snapped.

"Hold on, Lizzie, I'll just step outside for a minute," Raoul whispered.

She waited impatiently for him to leave the bedroom, then shouted, "I need to know where he is!"

"Lizzie, I wanted to tell you in person," Raoul insisted.

"It's too late for that now. You text me at four thirty in the morning that Ramon is gone and now you want to take it back?"

"Lizzie, I am sorry. It's been an awful day. Believe me, this isn't easy for me."

"What's not easy? Talking to me?" Lizzie shouted.

"Lizzie, Ramon is dead."

"*Dead?* How? Where?"

"His body was found in the desert in the Canyon Sin Nombre. I went out there today with my parents. I had to identify the body. It was horrible. His face . . . there was hardly anything left . . . The vultures, and coyotes . . ." Raoul broke off. "I had to identify him from his watch, his clothes, his hair . . ."

"Enough, stop, Raoul!" Lizzie cried.

"Lizzie, I'm so sorry. I don't know how to do these things, how to say them."

"You are a fucking idiot!" Lizzie agreed.

"I know. Do you want me to come over?" Raoul felt like a complete jerk.

"Yes!" Lizzie sobbed.

"I'll be right there."

12

FRIDAY, DECEMBER 20, 4:45 A.M.

As Raoul drove through the quiet predawn streets, his thoughts were in shambles. He had made a real mess of the conversation with Lizzie and now he had to go and see her to make up for it, even though he was conflicted about it. He felt attracted to Lizzie and had been jealous when Ramon brought her to the house for the first time. She was so glamorous, self-confident, and beautiful. Raoul felt loyal to his wife, Tina, but they had been married for fifteen years and had two children together. There wasn't much romance left. Ramon was the one with the exciting lifestyle. He went to fancy parties and art openings and people wrote newspaper articles about him. When he first showed up with this gorgeous, rich, young girlfriend, Raoul had just returned from working in the family roofing business and stank of tar.

Raoul took care of their parents and his kids in the small house they shared. Raoul had done everything right in his life. He had finished school and stayed out of trouble and helped his parents, while Ramon just dreamt up strange happenings and installations and got rewarded for them. Raoul's reward in life was more work, more responsibility, and his wife's constant complaint that they needed a bigger house.

Raoul knew he looked like his brother. They both had the sharp Indian features and the black hair. But where Ramon was smooth and confident in any company, Raoul often felt awkward and shy. Raoul had helped his brother with several installations, even though he didn't quite understand them. Of course Ramon's girlfriend was completely taboo, even in his mind, but now that he was gone . . .

He reached Lizzie's apartment building in an upscale part of town. Her light was on, the only one in the entire block. His heart skipped a beat in anticipation of seeing her. He was here to comfort her and make her feel better after her terrible shock. Maybe they could talk about Ramon, honor his memory. Who knew what would develop? Raoul parked his Toyota pickup truck and went upstairs.

FRIDAY, DECEMBER 20, 9:00 A.M.

Sheriff Deputy Lieutenant Thompson's office was absolutely packed. Thompson presided behind his huge, battered desk. Detective Andy Vincelli from the San Diego Police Department and Lieutenant Brian McInness from the US Border Patrol sat in the two visitor chairs in front of him. The two were a study in opposites.

Andy Vincelli, a plainclothes detective, wore a stylish gray three-piece suit with narrow lapels. It was his habit to run his fingers through his mid-length curly dark hair. He was slim and trim, and his lively dark eyes darted around the room.

In contrast to Vincelli, Brian McInness filled the entire visitor seat with his bulk. Not that one could have called him fat, but he was substantial. At six foot four, he towered over Vincelli and seemed to crush Deputy Ling. He wore his green uniform proudly and his movements were slow and deliberate, matching his size. Now he sat very straight, both of his heavy-duty steel-tipped boots planted firmly on the floor, hat on his lap. His red face with its bushy eyebrows was unreadable, but ready.

Along with Thompson's deputy, the rest of the visitors had to stand. These were Detective Henderson from the San Diego Police

Department and Dr. Chun, the medical examiner, who had performed the autopsy.

"Well, it's good we are all here together, so we can decide what to do about this mess," Thompson boomed. "Let's hear Dr. Chun's autopsy report first, and then go from there."

Dr. Chun cleared his throat. "The deceased has been identified by his brother Raoul as Ramon Matus, thirty-five years old, a resident of San Diego's Barrio Logan. According to the autopsy, the time of death was Wednesday, December eighteenth, between five and nine p.m. Cause of death was a gunshot to the head, with a .380-caliber bullet, most likely originating from a lightweight Beretta 84 Cheetah semiautomatic pistol. There was severe trauma to the face from the shot and from local wildlife.

"Death did not occur at the location where he was found in the Canyon Sin Nombre. Judging from the abrasions and blood pooling in the limbs, the death must have occurred shortly before his deposit in the canyon." He paused, looking around the room, as if to say, "It's your job to find out how he got there."

"I have brought the other forensics reports here. They state that there were no fingerprints or car tracks or blood samples. Any traces evaporated or seeped into the sandy ground," he concluded.

"Thank you, Dr. Chun," Thompson continued. "The body was found by a family hiking in the area on Thursday morning. They are presently staying at the Casa Del Zorro. The deceased carried with him a California driver's license and a letter addressed to him by a certain Jerome Schlesinger. He was wearing a gold watch and stylish leather loafers. We need to follow up on each of these pieces of evidence," he concluded.

Detective Vincelli took over: "We reviewed the victim's bank and phone records. On the day of his death, Ramon Matus withdrew twenty thousand dollars from his account at the Wells Fargo Bank at five forty-five p.m., just before the bank closed. We are getting his phone records for the night of his death. His cell phone is missing, and his family members said they'd tried to reach him unsuccessfully. We are still conducting interviews with the family. We searched the victim's studio apartment, but it yielded no helpful clues, except a large number of sketches and art books. However, we have posted surveillance."

"Thank you, Detective. McInness, what can you tell us?" Thompson interjected.

"The victim was an American citizen born in San Diego, but we are investigating a possible link to a drug cartel. The method of the execution-style killing fits within the pattern of the drug cartels. The large amount of money may point to a deal gone wrong or a blackmail attempt. We are presently working with our contacts in this area to find out if anything went down on Wednesday night. The Beretta .380-caliber murder weapon is a pistol frequently used by Mexican drug cartel hit men. Usually the weapons come from a US gun store."

"Thanks, McInness. My deputy, Mai Ling, over there, has taken on the task of talking to the family who found the body. She has also tried to speak to the sender of the letter in the victim's pocket, Jerome Schlesinger. He happens to be staying at the Casa Del Zorro at the moment. He is conducting a . . . what's it called, Mai?"

"A winter solstice retreat, Sir."

"Yes, that. The fact that he is here right now is an interesting coincidence. The victim may have intended to visit or meet with Mr. Schlesinger. Deputy Ling will follow up with him. She will also be your liaison to help coordinate the cooperation between our three departments. You will be able to contact her at any time with new information and she will keep you updated as well. So make sure you exchange all your contact information. We'll meet here again in three days."

Nods all around, but Detective Vincelli frowned.

"Just a couple of questions," Vincelli asked. "Shouldn't we be meeting earlier than three days from now? I know you are in charge here, Sheriff, and I don't want to tell you how to do your job, but in a murder investigation three days is a long time."

"We have to conduct the interviews and assemble the facts. We don't want to waste everybody's time before we have new information to tell you," Thompson said. He had to put this smart-aleck detective in his place. At least he realized who was in charge here. "What's your other question, Vincelli?"

Vincelli swallowed after his rebuke. "Why did the murderer take the money but leave the gold watch behind? If we assume it was a robbery, that doesn't make sense."

"We'll have to deal with that. But a lot about this murder doesn't make sense. Why was the victim in the desert in the first place and how did he get to the Canyon Sin Nombre? It's not an easy place to reach. I could think of more convenient places to dump a body. Someone had to carry him up there for quite a way. You can't just drive in and out," explained Thompson.

"The Canyon Sin Nombre isn't on any known route of either drug or migrant smuggling," said McInness.

"It's just a real interesting name," Ling said, but everybody ignored her.

"Well, unless there is something else, that's all for today then!" Thompson got up and everybody shook hands and chatted for a few minutes before they dispersed, leaving Thompson alone to contemplate the meeting.

He was quite pleased with himself. He thought it had gone very well. Ling would get to do all the footwork and paperwork and liaison with all the different departments involved. He'd be out of the loop, and in case something went wrong, he couldn't be blamed.

14

FRIDAY, DECEMBER 20, 11:00 A.M.

L izzie opened the door to Ramon's loft with her key. Without much thought, she ducked underneath yellow police tape to get in. Weak winter sunrays fell onto the wooden floor through the slants of closed blinds.

The studio looked as if Ramon had just left to get cigarettes or a coffee. A glass of wine stood half-empty on the counter. The platform bed was unmade, and a pair of jeans and a black T-shirt lay crumpled on the floor. Lizzie went to the desk and leafed through the papers in search of a letter, a message, something to provide a clue about what had happened. She only found bills, along with several invitations to art openings.

She walked over to his workspace, which took up the better part of the loft. Preliminary drawings for a new installation were tacked onto the wall. They involved dried and fresh flowers. She could not quite picture what the finished work would look like. A sound came from the door. Lizzie spun around, startled. A young man with fashionably spiked blond hair and a gray suit with narrow-cut pants stood in the doorway.

"Who are you? What are you doing here?" he called. She sized him up: about twenty-seven years old, fairly good-looking in a conventional way, but aware of it, and slightly cocky, though probably less self-confident than he appeared; definitely more bark than bite.

"What are *you* doing here?" she shouted back. "You are trespassing." *Don't give him an inch. Make sure he knows who he's dealing with.*

"Didn't you see the yellow police tape?"

"I have a right to be here," retorted Lizzie, ignoring his question. He wasn't going to get the satisfaction of dominating this conversation and criticizing her actions. Lizzie always got what she wanted. Her daddy had made sure of that.

"What gives you the right to be here?" he asked.

"I have a key. I'm the girlfriend of this loft's owner. What gives you the right to interrogate me?" Lizzie was not easily intimidated.

"Police Detective Henderson." He showed her his badge. "I have a few questions for you."

"Why are you here?" Lizzie asked.

"This apartment is under surveillance. What was your relationship with Ramon Matus?"

"I told you, I'm his girlfriend, and anything else is none of your business."

"It's police business. This is a murder investigation." He stepped closer and looked at her appraisingly. She saw him checking out her miniskirt, boots, and long blond hair.

"Murder? Ramon was not murdered. It was an accident."

"He was shot in the head. That usually doesn't happen by accident. Where were you on Wednesday night between five and nine p.m.?"

Lizzie stopped dead in her tracks. Ramon shot. In the head. She felt as if her head drained of blood and a clump formed in her stomach. This had to be the most brutal way to tell a loved one that her partner was murdered. Ramon had always felt invincible. She wanted to break down and cry. But she had to stay strong. She just didn't believe he was murdered. Balling her hands into fists and straightening her spine, Lizzie determined to get to the bottom of this.

"Am I a suspect now? I need an alibi?" she asked defiantly.

"We have to ask everybody who knew the victim."

"I was at a party. I have at least twenty witnesses."

"We'll need names."

"Fine," she said offhandedly.

"So you dated this Mexican guy?" Henderson wondered out loud.

This cocky detective wondered why she'd been dating a "Mexican guy," the stupid idiot. He thought she could have done better, probably even considered himself a candidate. As if she'd ever date a cop.

"He was not just 'some Mexican guy,' you ignorant fool. He was an emerging art star, an admired conceptual artist. I bet you don't even know what that means."

"Conceptual artist?" Henderson looked doubtful.

"Don't you guys do any research? Don't you do homework on the background of your victims?" Lizzie shot back contemptuously. She walked over to a bookshelf.

"Here, read this. There is an essay about Ramon's work in this catalogue. An art historian, Vega Stern, wrote it." She pulled out an exhibition catalogue and tossed it to Henderson.

"Vega Stern, that name sounds familiar," Henderson mumbled.

"She is fairly well known, but probably not in your circles," Lizzie remarked acidly. This cop was a fool. "Why was Ramon in the desert?" she asked.

Henderson didn't answer; instead he asked, "Does the name Jerome Schlesinger mean anything to you?"

"Jerome, Jerome . . . I have heard that name, but he's not an artist or collector."

"No, he's a new-age guru, author of a self-help book, teaching a retreat in the desert. Your boyfriend had a letter from him in his pocket."

"Ah yes, Jerome Schlesinger. Now I remember. He wrote that book *The Ten Laws of Spiritual, Mental, and Emotional Expansion*."

Now Henderson looked stumped.

"I bet you haven't read that one either. Where's he teaching?"

"At the Casa Del Zorro in Borrego Springs. A winter solstice retreat."

"Ramon must have been on his way to see him," concluded Lizzie.

"That's what we're trying to find out."

"Are we done here?" Lizzie asked impatiently. She was suddenly in a hurry to get home.

"I guess; I just need your contact information and—"

"And I am not allowed to leave town." Lizzie complied, giving him her address and phone number, smiling sweetly. She knew exactly what Henderson was thinking. Guys were too easy to read; it was ridiculous. All guys except Ramon. He was a mystery. And she was determined to solve it.

15

FRIDAY, DECEMBER 20, 11:00 A.M.

J erome Schlesinger sat in the middle of the conference room in meditation pose. He had removed all the furniture to create a quiet, empty space opening onto the rose garden of the Casa Del Zorro and its murmuring fountain. Sunlight filtered through green rosebushes and fell in flickering patterns onto the white carpet. All was peaceful, except for Jerome Schlesinger's thoughts.

Meditation did not come easily today. He just couldn't empty his mind. He thought about the upcoming winter solstice retreat he was going to teach. It was ridiculous to be nervous about it. He had lectured under much more stressful circumstances. His teaching was based on his book *The Ten Laws of Spiritual, Mental, and Emotional Expansion,* and he had plenty of examples to illustrate these laws. But the retreat group was small, only five students. That in itself was worrisome. Why only five?

His book had been published two years ago and the initial interest had already diminished to a trickle. Newer, more sensational self-help books had taken over his market share. He needed to write something new. In the meantime, he just had to relax and enjoy this beautiful setting. Make the best of this retreat. Law #8: *Enjoy the moment. It will never come back and it is all you have.* But the more he tried to calm down, the more peace of mind evaded him.

The Casa Del Zorro had given him a good deal to hold his retreat here. They were struggling as well, trying to keep the villas and guest rooms occupied. *The maintenance of this place must cost a fortune,* Schlesinger pondered, as he looked out on the immaculately trimmed roses. The resort administration was surely disappointed at the low turnout as well.

Jerome realized that he was contradicting another one of his own spiritual laws: Law #1: *Act, don't react.* He was reacting to his own nerves and the disappointing numbers with agitation. He should just accept and experience his uneasiness, without trying to avoid it. Law #3: *Don't try to avoid uncomfortable feelings. Observe and experience them fully.* Only then could he act freely.

What a perfect example, he realized. He could use this thought process tomorrow morning to introduce the retreat. Jerome smiled. His laws had proven themselves correct again. His nervousness evaporated as he began breathing deeply. He closed his eyes to enter a meditative state. But quiet contemplation was not to be. His wife and assistant, the attractive and much younger Hilde, entered.

"Hilde, I asked not to be disturbed," Jerome said, slightly annoyed.

"I know, dear, but this is important and unavoidable," she answered cheerfully.

"What is so important that it can't wait for half an hour?"

"The police."

Hilde held the door open to two police officers in uniform. One was large and fat enough to pop the buttons on his uniform shirt. He had a mustache, and his face was bright red. *High blood pressure,* Jerome thought. The other officer was a petite, pretty Asian woman. She looked much too young to be working for the police. *She should still be in high school,* he thought. Her sleek, black hair was gathered in a tight bun. She smiled at him. Jerome smiled back.

"What can I do for you, officers?" he asked pleasantly. *Act, don't react.*

"Are you Jerome Schlesinger?" the big man asked.

"Yes, I am. May I ask for your names?" *Act, don't react.*

"I'm Deputy Sheriff Thompson from the Borrego Springs Sheriff's Department and this is my assistant sheriff, Mai Ling. We have a few questions for you."

"Go right ahead," Jerome said encouragingly, as if this were the question-and-answer part of one of his seminars.

Thompson looked around the empty room uncomfortably. There were no chairs in sight. Jerome still sat on the floor in meditation pose, so Ling sat down cross-legged in front of him as if she hadn't done anything else all her life.

"Do you know Ramon Matus?" she asked.

"I know *of* him. I don't know him personally. Why?" *Act, don't react.*

Thompson ignored his question. "Where were you on Wednesday evening between five and nine p.m.?"

"I was right here at the Casa. My wife and I came here a couple of days before the retreat to settle in and prepare. Why? Did something happen?"

This time Ling continued: "Did you plan to meet Ramon Matus here?"

"I always wanted to meet him, but we never made specific plans."

"So you never met Matus and you never set up a meeting with him?"

"Correct. Although I very much hope to meet him in the future," confirmed Schlesinger.

"Well, it's too late for that now," said Thompson irritably, shifting from one foot to the other.

"Why is it too late to meet him?"

Again Thompson ignored him. "Do you have witnesses for Wednesday evening?" he barked.

"My wife and I went to dinner at Bertrand's. He can confirm we were there."

"Until nine p.m.?" boomed Thompson.

"Yes, we got back here around nine thirty, as my wife can confirm. Won't you tell me what this is all about?"

"We'll talk to your wife, but she is not much of an alibi," Thompson said dismissively.

"An alibi for what?"

"Why did you want to meet Ramon Matus?" Ling asked.

"He's a very interesting artist and a Yaqui Indian. He weaves Yaqui concepts and elements of the Yaqui worldview into his art in a subtle and subversive way. I wanted to talk to him about that. I'm researching Yaqui philosophy for my next book."

"Ramon Matus was killed on Wednesday evening. He had a letter from you in his pocket."

"Oh my God, that is terrible! What a horrible loss!" Jerome lost his composure and clutched his hands to his head.

"We found his body not far from here."

"Now I understand. You thought he came here to see me."

Ling nodded.

"I wish he had. Maybe I could have helped him. I would have tried my best to save his life. He was a very special and talented person. I admired him, or at least his work. I will do anything I can to help you find who did this." Schlesinger said, visibly upset.

"Did you receive any communication, call, or message from Matus in response to your letter?"

"No, nothing. I figured he just was not interested."

"We'll talk to your wife now. Please do not leave Borrego Springs for the next few days."

"I'm not planning to. I'm teaching a winter solstice retreat here."

"Yes, we know," said Thompson wearily, as Ling got up fluidly from the floor and closed her notebook.

16

FRIDAY, DECEMBER 20, 11:30 A. M.

On their way out, Thompson muttered to Ling, "I was getting tired of standing around this empty room talking to Mahatma Gandhi down on the floor."

Ling smiled and asked Hilde about their whereabouts on Wednesday evening. As expected, she confirmed what Jerome had said.

"Can we see a list of the retreat participants?" she added.

It was not a long list, only three names: Vega Stern, Betsy, and Bertrand, as Thompson noticed with surprise. His friend and restaurant owner Bertrand sometimes decided to quit the booze, and then tried whatever he could find as spiritual support in Borrego Springs. *That must be it*, Thompson concluded. Bertrand was desperate and here was a guru right in town, with plenty of room in his class. Ling noticed another familiar name.

"Vega Stern is on the list. She and her family found the body. We should talk to them," she suggested.

"Yes," Thompson agreed.

"They're staying right here at the Casa," Hilde offered helpfully. "We had another sign-up this morning. Her name is not on the list yet. A Liz Cantor from San Diego. And then we have a journalist, Paula

Patterson, from LA, who wants to write a story on Jerome for *Los Angeles Magazine*. We like the publicity, but we have to be careful not to disrupt the other participants," she explained, shuffling her papers.

"Thank you for your help," Ling said.

"May I ask what this is all about?" Hilde said to both of them.

"It's a murder investigation," Thompson answered in a tone clearly communicating that no further information would be forthcoming.

"Mai, you go and talk to Vega Stern." He suddenly felt extremely hungry and tired. "I'll talk to Bertrand."

17

FRIDAY, DECEMBER 20, 11:30 A.M.

Josefina sat in the small living room of their house, watching TV. She wasn't used to being idle, but she was still dazed from the trip to Anza-Borrego and from the shock of Ramon's death. She couldn't bring herself to go into the kitchen and cook, or to call her employer, Betsy, and explain. She told herself that her English wasn't good enough, but really she didn't want to talk about what had happened. She didn't want to say the words: *Ramon is dead.* That would make it too real, too final in her mind. She hadn't seen the body. Marcos and Raoul had done that. She could still hang on to a shred of doubt that maybe it was all a mistake.

Her grandchildren were with her. Fourteen-year-old Jaime sat on the sofa and ten-year-old Juan on a stuffed brown easy chair. They were doing homework or playing on their little Game Boys. Josefina couldn't tell the difference. They always had some electronic device in their hands, and their thumbs were tapping away at the buttons at lightning speed.

The boys hardly talked to Josefina. They were too absorbed in their own worlds. Juan didn't even want to speak Spanish anymore. "This is America!" he'd say proudly. "I am American, born and raised!" It made Josefina sad, but she understood. They wanted to be accepted in this country as equals, not as cheap laborers.

Fox News came on. Josefina wasn't really listening, but suddenly something the announcer said caught her ear: "The body of a young Mexican-American artist has been found in the Anza-Borrego Desert's Canyon Sin Nombre. The police are looking for witnesses who may have seen the victim on Wednesday evening between five and nine p.m. Ramon Matus, thirty-five, was a conceptual artist represented by the Ronald Cantor Gallery in Los Angeles's Bergamot Station. In a statement to the press, Ronald Cantor expressed the profound loss the art community is experiencing."

Here the face of Ronald Cantor came into view. Tanned and impeccably dressed in a light pin-striped suit and a wide silver tie, he looked gravely into the camera.

"Ramon was a good friend and an incredibly gifted artist. His death is not only a tragedy for the local art community, but for the international art world as a whole. He was on the cusp of becoming internationally recognized and appreciated. His conceptual artworks incorporated border issues in poetic installations, and he always acknowledged and grappled with his Native American Indian roots. Ramon may be gone, but his work endures. We are holding an exhibition of his art in his memory at the Cantor Gallery, opening tomorrow."

The camera cut back to the announcer, who now talked about the unemployment figures and the dismal state of the economy.

"Tina, kids! Ramon was on television," Josefina cried.

Tina entered the living room, drying her hands on an apron. The kids looked up for a moment and then, bored, went back to their electronic devices. Tina lingered.

"What did they say?" she asked.

"That Ramon's body was found in the desert and that his gallery will have a show of his work."

"Nobody told us about it. We should be at the opening," Tina stated. "Raoul at least should go. Where is he, anyway? I haven't seen him all day."

18

FRIDAY, DECEMBER 20, 12:00 NOON

L izzie sat on the bed with packed bags at her feet. She listened to the Fox News broadcast and her father's statement with a frown on her face. Immediately she picked up the phone and called his number.

"Dad!" she cried. "What are you doing?"

"Hi, sweetheart, did you see me on TV?" he answered cheerfully.

"Yes, I did, and I don't like it. How can you be so heartless? He isn't even in the ground yet and you're already exploiting his memory. That's such bad taste."

"Sweetheart, you still have a lot to learn. It's not bad taste, it's good business. A dead artist is the best publicity for a gallery."

"Dad, that's disgusting!"

"Sweetheart, I'm very sorry he had to die, especially in such a ghastly way, but now that he's dead we must forge the blade as long as it's hot, so to speak."

"Forge the blade? What are you talking about?"

"Sell his work, sweetheart. He had not exactly achieved stellar sales during his lifetime. Conceptual art is hard to sell. We are elevating Ramon's reputation and his prices now."

"Too bad he can't benefit from that!" Lizzie shot back sarcastically.

"That's indeed a shame, my dear. But we'll profit, as will his family, and just think of his legacy! Curators and collectors will think of him in a completely different light. He's in another league now. Not just another local artist tackling border issues."

"Dad, that's very unfair. He was never just a local artist with border issues. He was always much more."

"I know, sweetheart. You're a great fan of his work, but not everybody understood Ramon like you do. I agree with you; I always saw his potential. Now we have a chance to show the world what he was made off."

"How can you pull an exhibition together in such a short time?"

"I have accumulated quite a bit of inventory of Ramon's work. Since you two have been together, I've become the main collector of his art. It's easy to bring it out of storage and install it at the gallery. You should come to the opening. It looks beautiful."

"Dad, you're pathetic."

"Sweetheart, I know you're upset. I would be too—I am, actually. You need a little break, a vacation to calm your nerves. Come up and stay with us for a while."

"Dad, that's the last thing I want to do. But you're right; I need to get away. I'm going to the desert for a few days."

"Really? Where? Palm Springs? It will do you good. Let me know where you are, and if there's anything I can do for you . . . I love you!"

19

FRIDAY, DECEMBER 20, 12:00 NOON

Detective Henderson sat at his desk at the police station and thumbed through the catalogue Lizzie had given him. Vega Stern's essay about Ramon Matus didn't make any sense to him at all.

Ramon Matus does not only share the same last name with Don Juan Matus, who achieved fame in Carlos Castaneda's trilogy on 'The Teachings of Don Juan,' he is also of Yaqui Indian heritage. But here the similarities end. Matus's father emigrated from Mexico's Sonora district in the early 1980s and settled in San Diego, where he opened a roofing business. His two sons, Ramon and Raoul, were born in the United States. While Castaneda's Don Juan is a sorcerer of questionable authenticity, Ramon Matus is an artist of genuine uniqueness.

"Genuine uniqueness"? *What the heck.* Henderson doubted it would be helpful in solving this case. He was just doing his "homework," as Lizzie had put it. Maybe his boss, Vincelli, would be impressed that he had bothered to do some research into the victim's background. He had even bought Jerome Schlesinger's book *The Ten Laws of Spiritual, Mental, and Emotional Expansion.* It lay on his desk right in front of him. It looked like it would be even more work to read than this short essay, so he ploughed on through the catalogue.

Matus's Yaqui heritage has piqued the curiosity of collectors and art critics alike who seek the magical mystery in his work and mistake him for a New Age shaman. Matus, however, is a thoroughly modern conceptual artist who has left the "Indian romanticism and nostalgia" far behind while at the same time not denying his origins.

The assemblage Deer Target *is a typical example of Matus's ambivalent relationship with his heritage. Matus equipped a deer mask, which plays an important role in the sacred Yaqui Deer Dance, with a blinking red light used by bicyclists at night, right in the middle of the deer's forehead. The addition of modern technology to the mask turns it from a sacred totem into a target. The stealthy deer becomes supremely visible and can easily turn into a victim of hunters. The installation also updates and targets ancient Yaqui traditions, and has caused some friction with certain Elders.*

A deer mask with a red light? It sounded like Rudolph-the Red-nosed-Reindeer to Henderson. He sighed and continued.

Matus's 2005 installation Sands of Time *was part of the exhibition* Local Landscapes *at the California Center for the Arts Museum in Escondido. It consisted of a monochromatic, sand-colored space. A funnel extended from the ceiling to the middle of the room. A fine stream of sand trickled steadily from the funnel onto the floor, creating the impression of a walkable, large hourglass. The sand accumulated continuously during the exhibition, and what amounted to only a small pile on the floor in the beginning grew and began to fill the room after a few weeks. It made the passage through the space more and more difficult as visitors struggled over the shifting mounds of sand. The steady trickle was a poetic reminder of the passage of time and all that accumulates with it in our lives, our minds, and on our planet.*

"A poetic reminder of the passage of time?" Henderson mumbled to himself and checked his watch. How much more time should he devote to this esoteric nonsense?

The sand can eventually engulf and threaten us. The expanding deserts, created by drought caused by global warming, may be one of the layers of meaning of this work. The immediate experience of struggling through the shifting sand could be akin to the environment Mexican migrants find themselves in when they try to cross the border and the desert in search of work and some dignity in their lives, like the one experienced by Ramon Matus's father.

Ramon Matus was a first generation American, Henderson thought. His father made the journey across the border.

Ramon Matus's installation of the golden and silver-winged tennis shoes also pays homage to the migrants' plight. In one of his conceptual happenings, the artist and a group of friends and volunteers distributed rocks wrapped in red ribbons as directional markers in the Anza-Borrego desert to help migrants find their way to safety.

Vincelli walked into the office. "What are you reading, Henderson?" he asked casually.

"Some stuff about our victim. Listen to this: '*Ramon Matus cannot be reduced to a glorified activist and political spokesperson of illegal immigrants. His work has too many layers of meaning and poetic power. He tries to lead us beyond the rational and descriptive into the realm of poetry and pure imagery, where we have to grope around for lack of landmarks and recognizable directions.*'

"Yes, I'm groping around, that's for sure. How is that going to help us solve the case?" Henderson said with exasperation.

"Calm down, Henderson. It never hurts to have a little background information. That sounds pretty deep," assured Vincelli.

"Well, then take a look at this background information. A two-hundred-and-fifty-page book by our first suspect, Jerome Schlesinger. *The Ten Laws of Spiritual, Mental, and Emotional Expansion.*"

Vincelli took the book and opened it randomly. "'*Don't just avoid uncomfortable emotions. Observe, investigate, and experience them fully. Then they often disappear.*' I suggest you read this whole book and investigate your feelings about it." Vincelli laughed.

"Brilliant idea, boss. It may provide valuable insight into one of our suspects," Henderson said in mock seriousness.

"At this point everybody is a potential suspect," said Vincelli, as he sat down behind his desk and loosened his stylish gray tie.

"Even the girlfriend, Lizzie Cantor?"

"Especially the girlfriend. You know that domestic strife is the most common motive for murder."

"They didn't even live together."

"You fancy her, don't you? You met her in the victim's studio."

"It wasn't a studio, more like a loft or something, with a big work space."

"Well, he was an artist, so I think it's reasonable he had a work space. I think we should interview Lizzie Cantor again. Together this time."

"Okay, I'll bring her in," Henderson volunteered quickly. Vincelli looked up with a small grin.

"Here's the report from Deputy Ling about their interview with Schlesinger. He claims he never met Matus, but he was staying at the Casa Del Zorro, only a few miles from the location where the victim was found. Why did Matus carry his letter? It doesn't make sense."

"No, it doesn't, but according to this essay, 'Matus was trying to lead us beyond the rational . . .'"

"Is that what it says? If that's true, then we're going to have to hire a medium to solve the case," Vincelli concluded sarcastically. "But, so far, I've never encountered a case that couldn't be cracked with logic and luck."

"We could try a guru instead of a medium, since we already have one sitting around as a person of interest."

"You want to bring him in? We have to cooperate with the Sheriff's Department in Borrego Springs. They're in charge out there, and we cover the city."

"I think Ling's report will suffice. I'm not going to interview him cross-legged on the floor in my socks," Henderson protested.

"In that case, we might have to make do with logic and rational thinking."

20

FRIDAY, DECEMBER 20, 12:00 NOON

Mai Ling found the Stern family eating lunch in the Fox Bistro, an informal bar and dining room overlooking the pool and shady eucalyptus trees. Thompson had excused himself from the interview, which was fine with Ling. The Sterns were listening to a gray-haired pianist singing a jazzy tune. He was one of the entertainers invited by La Casa Del Zorro during the winter holiday season to stay for a few days and enjoy the amenities in exchange for providing entertainment in the lobby and lounge.

> *"We are living in the house of the fox*
> *Where time stands still day after day*
> *Where the city is far and the moon stands high*
> *Next to diamond stars in a velvet sky*
> *Where the cactus blooms and the land is dry."*

Ling waited patiently until the polite applause died down. She then approached the Sterns' table and apologized for the interruption. The two boys sat behind huge Shirley Temple drinks with big red maraschino cherries, and Vega and her husband drank red wine.

She introduced herself, and the Sterns invited her to sit down and have a drink with them.

"Just water—I'm on duty," she insisted.

"Do you have to work through the holidays?" asked Vega.

"With a murder investigation, there is no way I will get any time off," Ling said.

"You want to know how we found the body?" Vega guessed. "It was actually my son Stevie who found him."

Stevie nodded importantly. "The birds were picking his eyeballs out," he confirmed gravely.

"Do you know who the victim was?" asked Ling.

"We didn't know it at the time, but we heard in the news that it was Ramon Matus, the artist. My husband and I were just talking about him. We knew him, superficially; he was at the opening of *Local Landscapes*. He was one of the artists in the exhibition. I wrote a short essay about his work for the catalogue."

"You did?" Ling asked, surprised.

"Yes, I'm an art historian and write essays about many artists."

"Can you tell me about your impressions of Matus at the opening? What was he like?"

"He was very good-looking," Vega began, glancing over at her husband, who shook his head. "He had a stillness about him that was very appealing. He seemed to look through you, or at least through the outer layers, with his black eyes.

"At the opening everybody was chatting and sipping wine, looking around to see who else was there. Ramon had presence, but he didn't say much. I asked him about his process of making art and he considered my question for a long time. I had almost given up waiting for an answer, when he suddenly said, 'I can't explain my process. I just do what I'm compelled to do.' He added nothing else after that. His installations are fascinating, but it was also his magnetic personality that made them so compelling. If I did the same installation, nobody would take it seriously, but from him, they had credibility." Vega paused.

"Where and when did you interview him for your essay?" Ling asked, while writing in her notebook.

"I went to his studio a few weeks before the exhibition. It seemed like he didn't really trust me or couldn't quite open up to me. I don't understand why he would hold back. I was writing about him and it was in his interest to tell me about himself and his work. He got very animated when he talked about the desert and the installations he did out here, like the wrapped rocks. He clearly enjoyed it and felt that it was useful and visually intriguing."

"Did he mention any current desert installations to you?"

"No, just the wrapped rocks, an installation he did earlier in the year. It was documented in the *Local Landscapes* exhibition."

"Didn't you talk about anything personal besides his work?"

"We talked about his family, particularly his father, Marcos, who emigrated from Mexico. Ramon obviously respected and admired him. He said he was close to his family."

Ling looked down to take notes.

"And you're also participating in Jerome Schlesinger's winter solstice retreat?"

"Yes, that's why we're here, actually. We arrived a couple of days early to make a little holiday of it," Vega said.

"Do you know of any connection between Ramon Matus and Jerome Schlesinger?"

"I don't know about any connection, but I think they would get on famously, if they ever met," ventured Vega.

"Why do you say that?"

"I know Ramon's work and read Schlesinger's book. They have certain similarities and common interests."

"Funny you would say that," observed Ling. "Because we did find a connection between Ramon Matus and Jerome Schlesinger." Ling looked closely at Vega after making this statement. Vega stared back at her blankly. Then a look of comprehension appeared on her face.

"There are too many connections," she blurted out.

Greg put a hand on his wife's arm. He looked alarmed. "Vega, don't say anything else," he warned her.

Ling looked at him. "Why not, Mr. Stern?"

"Is this an interview or an interrogation, Deputy Ling?" Greg shot back. "If it is an interrogation, you need to tell us, and we'll bring in a lawyer."

"No need for that, but I have to ask you, where were you on Wednesday night between five and nine o'clock?"

"We were here, the whole family. We went to Bertrand's for an early dinner and then took a walk looking at the stars. After that we went to bed," Greg answered.

"You went to Bertrand's? Did you see anybody there?"

"Yes, Jerome and Hilde Schlesinger. They were there for dinner as well."

"What time did you see them?"

"It must have been around six thirty or seven. They came a little after us."

"How long were you there?"

"We left at eight thirty and got back to the Casa Del Zorro around nine," Greg said.

"Do you know the Schlesingers?"

"No, we just met them," Vega said.

"How did Ramon die?" Greg asked.

"He was shot."

Vega gasped. "What a terrible waste of talent and potential!" she exclaimed.

Ling pondered her reaction as she looked from husband to wife.

That's exactly what Jerome Schlesinger said, Ling thought.

21

FRIDAY, DECEMBER 20, 1:00 P.M.

Vega and Greg sat in deck chairs by the turquoise swimming pool and watched Stevie and Daniel splash around in the water. One of them pretended to be a shark chasing the other.

"Do you remember Ramon Matus from the museum opening?" Vega asked Greg.

"Yes. He seemed a bit aloof," recalled Greg.

"He did seem to hold back, even when I went to his studio," confirmed Vega.

"When he did his wrapped rocks installation here in the desert, did he ever meet with migrants and talk to them? Did the rocks actually help anybody?" Greg, always the pragmatist, asked.

"I asked him the same question. He said he had talked to many illegal immigrants and knew a lot of them personally, but he wasn't sure if his rocks had actually provided any guidance to anybody in the desert, if they had been useful as signposts."

"No measurable success," concluded Greg, the scientist.

"Not in that regard, but it was successful artistically."

"What was successful about it, if it never actually helped anybody?"

"Okay, you want the art historical explanation? Art isn't supposed to be utilitarian, or else it wouldn't be art. It would be social work or political activism."

Greg nodded impatiently.

"In this piece the rocks were wrapped like gifts, which is a role of art, metaphorically speaking. It's a gift that's not tangible, but it makes us see things we haven't seen before; it makes us feel emotions we haven't felt; it makes us see the world in a new way," Vega said.

"And the stones did all that?" Greg asked.

"Yes, I think they did."

"How did Ramon's studio look?" Greg shifted gears, obviously not keen on another art lecture.

"What you'd expect. A hodgepodge of objects: some ceremonial masks, drawings, rocks, different materials like sand and flowers. It wasn't like a typical artist's studio, because there were no paintings. Ramon did a lot of small sand models of spaces and installations. Everything in the large studio was ephemeral. It felt as if the artist living there could pick up at any time and leave."

"Why would he want to leave?"

"I don't know his motives. He was smart, maybe too smart. Maybe he thought I couldn't follow what he was really thinking."

"He underestimated you," said Greg.

"Thanks for saying that, but I think he felt he lived in such a different realm, and thought on such a different level, infused with the Yaqui Indian philosophy, that I couldn't possibly understand."

"Why be an artist, if you don't believe that even an art historian and art writer can follow you?" Greg asked.

"Good point," Vega conceded. "I remember one thing he said. I didn't put it in the essay, because it was so cryptic: 'The desert allows you to hear your own thoughts, but it also swallows them.'"

"Not only cryptic, but prophetic," confirmed Greg. "The desert swallowed him."

"Ramon also said that conceptual art doesn't only make us think, it also makes us aware of our thinking process, and that's even more important."

"If art leads to some self-awareness, it's a step in the right direction," admitted Greg.

The boys had by now abandoned the pool and sat in the hot tub.

"The police think there's a connection between Ramon and Jerome Schlesinger," considered Greg.

"I don't know," said Vega with a sigh. "It seems we're going around in circles."

The boys came over, wrapped in towels. They announced that they were hungry, which concluded Greg and Vega's conversation.

22

FRIDAY, DECEMBER 20, 1:00 P.M.

O ne of the Casa Del Zorro employees had to drive Deputy Ling in a resort shuttle bus back to the Sheriff's Department, because Sheriff Thompson had taken the patrol car.

She felt very confused. There were too many points of connection between Ramon Matus, Vega Stern, and Jerome Schlesinger. Vega knew Ramon, had written an essay about him, found his body, and stayed only a few miles from where he died. She was a participant in a retreat with Schlesinger, whose letter was in Ramon's pocket. In Ling's mind, there was only one explanation for these coincidences: Matus had come to the desert to meet with Schlesinger or Vega Stern or both.

The Stern family and the Schlesingers both had dinner at Bertrand's on the night Matus was killed, but Vega claimed they didn't know each other. Admittedly, Borrego Springs was a very small place, and it was not unusual to run into the same people over and over again. After all, there were only a limited number of restaurants to choose from.

Then there was the issue of the $20,000 Matus had withdrawn on the day of his death. Where was the money? What had been its purpose? They would have to explore the possibilities of a drug deal gone wrong, blackmail, or expensive art materials.

Maybe Matus's brother, Raoul, would know if Ramon was involved in any kind of drugs. Ling had talked to him in the car on the way to the morgue, but Raoul had been very quiet and hesitant. She had attributed this to the shock of his brother's death, but maybe there was more to it. Maybe Raoul knew more than he let on. Then there was the question of why Ramon's gold watch hadn't been taken by the killers, when they took the money and his wallet. They'd have to check into the make and value of the watch. Vincelli had brought it up at the meeting, but Thompson had brushed him aside.

Ling sighed. She had to write up her report for Thompson and the other agencies. Then she had to read their reports and redistribute them. It was four days before Christmas. She'd planned to go home and visit her parents in Los Angeles for the holiday, but she knew that wasn't going to happen; there was no way she could get away. She pictured her Christmas holiday in her small office in the Sheriff's Department, bent over files and reports. She was okay with that. This case was her first big break.

She'd come straight out of the Police Academy and hadn't expected a high-profile case on her first assignment. Already she was making valuable contacts with the Border Patrol and the San Diego Police Department. This could only be helpful for her career—if she did well. Thompson gave her an amazing level of independence and responsibility, allowing her to be the liaison between the different agencies. That kind of delegation was way beyond her level of experience, and she was worried about doing everything right. This case could launch or end her career. She appreciated the opportunity, but she knew Thompson had not entrusted her with the task out of a belief in her competence, but rather out of laziness. True to form, when she got back to the office, he was still at lunch.

23

FRIDAY, DECEMBER 20

T he journalists started to descend on Borrego Springs. The local
newspaper, the *Borrego Sun,* was the first to pick up the story. It
published only twice a month, with an edition of four thousand. Then
journalists from San Diego and Los Angeles arrived. They populated
La Casa Del Zorro and some of the motels. They filled the tables at
Bertrand's restaurant. They climbed the desert hills on their way to the
Canyon Sin Nombre. They took pictures of the desert trails and valleys
and filled the Southern California newspapers with headlines like
"Death in the Desert," "Mysterious Mexican Artist Murdered," or even
"Mexican Murder Mystery." One newspaper claimed "Big-name Artist
Found in Canyon-Without-Name."

That was a bit of an exaggeration, but it sounded good. They
published pictures of the badlands and canyons, to pique the interest
of their readers in the city. Murder tourists decided to visit the exotic
desert at their doorstep for the holidays, taking day trips to the Visitor
Center and doing some of the easier hikes. The Borrego Springs
Chamber of Commerce was delighted about this windfall. To celebrate
the occasion, they added extra decorations to the holiday display on
Christmas Circle.

The papers published photos of a romantic-looking Ramon with long, black hair and intense eyes next to the desert landscapes. It was a successful combination, which sold papers and made it into the social media and online news sources. The journalists pestered the sheriff and asked Jerome, Hilde, and Vega about Ramon. Jerome cautiously savored the media attention, and Bertrand served up loads of sauer-braten, spätzle, and bratwurst, glad to have finally found an apprecia-tive audience.

When there were no new developments after a couple of days, the media attention faded as quickly as it had begun. Borrego Springs returned to being a sleepy desert town.

24

FRIDAY, DECEMBER 20, 1:30 P.M.

Detective Henderson repeatedly rang the bell and knocked on the door of Lizzie's apartment. After five minutes of his futile efforts, the door across the hallway opened and a middle-aged woman in a patterned housedress stepped out.

"You can bang as loud as you want," she said. "She won't open."

Henderson looked at her in surprise.

"She's gone. I saw her drive off in her little blue convertible about half an hour ago, all dolled up, with her suitcase and everything."

Henderson realized he had found the perfect eyewitness. This woman would probably be able to supply the exact make, color, and cut of Lizzie's outfit at her departure.

"Are you sure? She was supposed to stay in town."

"Well, she's gone, like I said. Around one o'clock she took off."

This was right after his encounter with Lizzie at Ramon's loft. He cursed under his breath.

"You from the police?" the woman asked.

"Detective Henderson, San Diego Police," he introduced himself and held up his badge.

"I read in the papers about the murder," she continued. "The artist, Ramon Matus—he was here."

"I understand Liz Cantor was his girlfriend."

"Yes, he visited here quite a bit. But he was here this morning. Really early in the morning."

"That's impossible, Mrs. . . ."

"Shmelkes, Mrs. Shmelkes. Would you like to come in?" she offered helpfully.

They entered her small apartment and proceeded straight to the kitchen, which had a window looking onto the street right above the building's entrance.

"Ramon Matus died on Wednesday, two days ago."

"I'm telling you, he was here this morning, around five a.m. I can't sleep so well anymore. I got up early and I was making myself a cup of tea in the kitchen. It was still dark, of course, but I heard him come up the stairs. He didn't ring the doorbell. Went right in. He left around eight o'clock. I know because I was listening to 'All Things Considered' on NPR."

"You saw him leave the building?"

"Yes, he walked down the street in this direction." She pointed toward the right.

"Did you see his face?"

"No, but I recognized his long hair blowing in the breeze. It was him all right. I've seen him often enough."

"How often have you seen him?"

"Oh, many times, when he came here to visit his girlfriend."

"What was he wearing?" Henderson furiously took notes in his notebook, his mind racing.

"He wore jeans and a jacket. It was hard to see details. It was so early and barely light. But I saw his hair and the way he walked." Mrs. Shmelkes was obviously very pleased with herself. She seemed to enjoy the confused look on the young policeman's face.

"Did he leave alone, or was Ms. Cantor with him?"

"Oh no, he left alone. Lizzie Cantor only left the apartment around one o'clock with her suitcase, as I told you before," Mrs. Shmelkes answered with satisfaction.

Henderson scribbled in his notebook.

"Are you prepared to come to the station and make a statement about this?" he asked.

"Of course. It'll be my pleasure," she responded cheerfully. "Let me just get a coat."

Henderson smiled. Mrs. Shmelkes was obviously expecting to be the star witness in a murder case.

25

FRIDAY, DECEMBER 20, 2:00 P.M.

Detective Vincelli was similarly disappointed when he arrived at the Matus house in Barrio Logan to ask Raoul questions about his brother Ramon.

"I haven't seen my husband since last night," Raoul's wife, Tina, told him. She had invited Vincelli in and they sat at the kitchen table, which was covered by a colorful vinyl tablecloth. Tina offered him a cup of coffee and he accepted. It was strong and fragrant.

"Is he at work?" asked Vincelli.

"No, they haven't seen him at the shop, and he's not answering his cell phone. He had a big roofing job this week. His father had to fill in." Tina's hand holding the coffee cup trembled. Her eyes searched around the kitchen, as if she could find her missing husband there.

"How was the relationship between Ramon and Raoul?" Vincelli asked.

"They were very different, even though they looked so similar. Raoul works in his father's roofing business. He smears tar on people's houses. He has to feed a family and we live with his parents, while Ramon led this glamorous life, traveled to galleries and museums, had a pretty young girlfriend. But Raoul was always loyal, admired his brother and helped him with his happenings whenever he could. Even though I don't think he quite understood what Ramon was actually doing."

"Tell me about the kind of person Ramon was."

"He was always nice and friendly when he came here to the house on holidays or for the kids' birthdays. He brought them little gifts he'd made. Wooden figures he'd decorated with feathers and strings, or drawings. But I knew he wasn't really all here. His mind was somewhere else. He'd sit with us at the dinner table, but his answers often sounded as if he was thinking about something completely different."

"What about the interaction between Raoul and him?"

"They were brothers. Raoul adored Ramon. I don't know how to say it, but Raoul is more ordinary than Ramon. That's maybe not a good word. I always know what Raoul is thinking. With Ramon I never did. Except now I really don't know what's going on with Raoul either. He was gone when I woke up this morning. I'm afraid Raoul is very upset about Ramon's death. I'm worried he could do something stupid." Tina's finger traced the flower pattern on the tablecloth, trying to formulate her thoughts.

"If you're worried about him, we can issue a missing person alert after 24 hours," Vincelli offered.

"Yes. Maybe. I just hope he won't be mad at me for doing it." Tina twisted a dish towel in her hands.

"Do you have any idea where he could be?"

"Maybe across the border. We have family in Baja."

"I have one more question about Ramon. Do you know if he did any drugs?"

"I wouldn't know. Raoul probably would, but I can't imagine Ramon doing heavy drugs. He wanted to be aware and conscious of the world around him. He wanted to understand things deeply, sharpen his senses, not dull them. He hardly even touched alcohol. Maybe a glass of wine at dinner, but never more. Raoul, he sometimes gets drunk. I know there are times when he just wants to forget about everything. Us, and the business, and this little house. He goes and drinks with his buddies until he passes out, and afterward he's okay again. But not Ramon."

"Thank you for your frank replies. You're very perceptive, Mrs. Matus!"

"Am I? Nobody's ever said that to me."

"We'll do our best to find your husband. Do you have a recent picture of him?"

Tina went to find a picture while Vincelli stared at the purple and orange flowers on the vinyl tablecloth.

26

FRIDAY, DECEMBER 20, 4:00 P.M.

F our o'clock in the afternoon and four in the morning are the quietest hours in Borrego Springs. At four in the afternoon people are resting from their hikes, getting ready for happy hour, closing up shop for the day. Four in the morning was too early even for the maintenance workers in the gardens of the resort or the state park.

Bertrand usually enjoyed this quiet time. He stood behind the bar of his restaurant polishing glasses, which he'd need once he opened at five for happy hour and dinner. Right now, he kept the lights turned off and worked in the half darkness. The afternoon sunshine came in low through the glass entrance doors.

He was in bad shape. He knew it and there was not much he could do about it. During his twenty-two years in Borrego Springs, Bertrand had experienced plenty of ups and downs. They came in waves, and all he could do was ride them out. Sometimes he thought about leaving, going to a big city, where he could disappear into the crowd. But what was he going to do there? Open another restaurant? He was too old and tired to start over.

Bertrand glanced at his certificate from the Institute Gastronomique in Strasbourg, France, which hung framed on the wood-paneled wall behind the bar. He was a certified French chef and maybe he could find work in someone else's restaurant, where he didn't have to worry about the bills and customers who couldn't even tell the difference between French fries and potato chips.

With a dull sound, the glass in his hands splintered. The shards cut his skin and blood dripped all over the counter. He had squeezed too hard. Cursing, he cleaned up the glass pieces and placed Band-Aids over his cuts. He poured himself a glass of whiskey to keep his hands from shaking.

He had signed up for the retreat at La Casa Del Zorro out of desperation. He'd do anything for a little peace of mind. Anything—even bear the mockery of the deputy sheriff and whoever else was going to find out about it. His past had caught up with him again, as it did periodically. He knew from previous episodes that his nightmares would subside again eventually, but while he was in it, the turmoil was almost unbearable.

The little bell at the front door rang as someone entered the dim restaurant.

"We're still closed," Bertrand called out in his French accent. He was in no shape for customers.

"Bertrand, are you all right?"

Brian McInness from the Border Patrol loomed over him in the semidarkness.

"McInness, what brings you here?" Bertrand asked feebly.

"Are you okay? You look like a ghost. What's happened to your hand? You're bleeding." McInness leaned over the counter. Bertrand tried to hide his hand behind his back.

"I'm fine, just a little cut. Would you like something to drink?" Bertrand hoped to distract him.

"Just a beer maybe. I have some questions for you."

Bertrand's mind worked feverishly while he drew the beer. McInness and he had an agreement. Bertrand kept his eyes and ears open in the restaurant and bar about goings-on along the border. He reported strange customers with strong accents and a lot of money. In exchange, the law left him in peace. And a little peace was all Bertrand craved.

"I haven't seen or heard anything lately." He placed the foaming cold glass in front of McInness.

"Try to remember last Wednesday night. Who was here? What did people talk about?"

Bertrand thought for a moment. He remembered that night.

"There were a few guests from the Casa Del Zorro. The blond woman with her family. The older guy, who's teaching the retreat with his wife. Nice sort of person," he added unnecessarily.

"Who was at the bar after hours?"

"The usual locals; I closed up early around eleven."

"Any customers from the other side of the border? Any friends from the cartel?"

"Let me think." Bertrand felt beads of sweat form on his upper lip. He hoped McInness wouldn't see them in the dim light.

"Take your time, Bertrand, this is important."

McInness and Bertrand had known each other for years. Bertrand knew he was odd in this environment, with his chipped tooth and French accent, but the locals had gotten used to him over the years and stopped wondering what he was doing in their little community, French cooking certificate and all. Hopefully after all this time, McInness had gotten used to him as well, and trusted him more than he doubted him.

"There were two guys I've never seen before," Bertrand began. "They didn't say much, and they might have been tourists for the Christmas holiday."

"Can you describe them? Did they have an accent?"

"They wore jeans and windbreakers. They were in their mid-thirties."

"Were they a couple? What did they drink?"

"No, they weren't gay. They drank beer, and for holiday-makers they were pretty quiet."

"Accents?"

"I don't think so. You know it is hard for me to detect accents when people speak English. I have one myself."

"Were they waiting for someone?"

"I don't know. They were just here for happy hour. They left around six thirty."

"Would you recognize them?"

"I think so."

"We'll have you look through some photo albums of our friends from the cartels."

"The cartel members don't come in here for beer," Bertrand argued.

"They could have been low-level couriers or messengers. You know what happened on Wednesday night?"

"Yes, an artist was killed in the Canyon Sin Nombre."

"Have you been there lately?"

"I stay well away from that place."

"Good man, Bertrand. Thanks for the beer."

Bertrand watched him go. His injured hand throbbed.

27

FRIDAY, DECEMBER 20, 4:00 P.M.

A shadow fell on Lizzie's face as she was dozing in a deck chair by La Casa Del Zorro's pool. She wore a blue string bikini and large sunglasses. The winter sun felt good on her pale skin. She already felt much more relaxed, soaking up the warmth with every breath. Despite his heartlessness, her father had been right. She needed a vacation.

Lizzie blinked to see who obstructed the sun. Three figures loomed over her. One was bulky and huge and wore a sheriff's hat. The second was Detective Henderson, and the third was a slim, petite Asian woman. She hardly cast any shadow at all.

"Gentlemen, would you mind stepping out of my sun?" she said lazily.

"Liz Cantor, you weren't supposed to leave the city. Would you rather come with us to the Sheriff's Department and answer some questions?" Henderson said pompously.

"Oh please, just sit down and get on with your questions, if they're all that important," Lizzie suggested with a sigh.

"Why did you leave San Diego?" Henderson insisted, a little less sure of himself.

"What's the harm? You found me anyway."

"Ms. Cantor, is there somewhere private we can talk?" interceded the small Asian woman, apparently trying to ease the tension.

"You're with the police too?" Lizzie asked her.

"Sheriff's Deputy Mai Ling." She held up her badge.

"All right, let's sit in the rose garden, if it's that official and all," Lizzie relented. She swung her bare legs to the side of the deck chair and slipped into a pair of flip-flops.

"Don't you have a wrap or something?" Henderson asked irritably.

"If you insist." Lizzie pulled on an oversized white shirt and led them along the garden paths to a table in the cool and quiet rose garden, where the stone fountain gurgled in the background.

"Why did you come here?" Henderson asked after they sat down at a decorative wrought-iron table.

"I needed a break, a little vacation. Even my father said so. It's been very stressful and upsetting to process my boyfriend's violent death. Which you, Detective, conveyed to me in a particularly brutal way."

"You chose to come to the Anza-Borrego Desert and signed up for Schlesinger's retreat to process his death?" Henderson asked incredulously.

"I need the relaxation," Lizzie sighed with a dramatic flutter of her eyelashes and a flip of her long hair.

"Enough, Missy." Deputy Sheriff Thompson actually brought his fist down onto the delicate wrought-iron table.

Lizzie looked at him with surprise.

"Give us straight answers or we'll haul you off to the police station."

Lizzie shot him an appraising look. This sheriff really meant business.

"I signed up for the retreat because I wanted to find out why Ramon came to the desert."

"Thank you for answering honestly," said Thompson. "So you had no idea why he came here?"

"Obviously not."

"Do you have any idea why Ramon Matus withdrew twenty thousand dollars from his account?"

"I didn't know he had that much."

"Did he sell much of his work?"

"You have to ask my father. He was his art dealer. He'd know how much Ramon sold. I expect it wasn't astronomical. Conceptual art is hard to sell. Even though Ramon was developing a following, showed in museum exhibits, and got write-ups, conceptual art doesn't bring in much money. My father represents well-known conceptual artists like John Baldessari and Ed Ruscha. Ramon was far from their level."

"Do you know what Matus was working on when he died?" asked Henderson.

"You saw the drawings in his studio. It looked like an installation with heaps of flowers . . ."

"Like a funeral," Ling remarked.

They sat in silence for a moment, letting that statement sink in.

"Did Ramon do drugs?" Henderson finally asked.

"Not that I knew of," Lizzie said evasively.

"You seemed hesitant about Ramon's drug use." Ling sat on the edge of her iron chair. She looked very uncomfortable.

"Ramon went south periodically, to Baja and Sonora. He was searching for his Yaqui roots. He may have done peyote or mushrooms, because he came back with strange stories and surreal ideas after those trips. But I don't know for sure. I didn't go with him," Lizzie said.

"Do you know any of his contacts in Mexico?" Thompson's booming voice made Lizzie flinch.

"No, I don't. That was his world. I didn't participate in that part of his life. But maybe Raoul would know, or even their father, although I doubt it. The older Mr. Matus never returned to Mexico. He was done with that."

"Talking about Raoul, he's gone missing. Any idea where he could be?" Detective Henderson said casually.

For a split second, Lizzie's face registered shock. Then she got a hold of herself and shot back calmly:

"Maybe you should ask his wife."

"She reported him missing. She's worried about him."

"That's not good. I'm sorry, but I've no idea where he could be."

"There is one more question we'd like to clear up," Henderson continued. "A neighbor in your apartment building claims she saw your boyfriend Ramon visiting you very early this morning and leaving again around eight. She claims she saw him visiting before and recognized him. Can you shed some light on that?"

"That old hag Shmelkes. She's just a busybody with nothing better to do than to spy on us behind her curtains."

"That doesn't answer our question," Thompson said.

"I don't know what she's talking about."

"Ms. Cantor, let me warn you, if you know anything that can shed light on either Ramon Matus's death or Raoul Matus's disappearance, and you withhold it from us, you are incriminating yourself and you are obstructing a murder investigation. Is that clear?" Deputy Sheriff Thompson stated firmly.

Lizzie swallowed. "It was Raoul who came to see me early this morning."

"What was Raoul doing in your apartment before dawn this morning?"

"He was comforting me."

"Comforting?" Thompson asked.

"Don't be so sarcastic. He'd told me on the phone that Ramon died. I was upset, and he came over for company. So I wouldn't have to be alone."

"To comfort you?"

"How many times do you have to ask the same question? I don't have to tell you anything about my private life." Lizzie was furious. She was not going to be intimidated by this bully sheriff.

"Whatever you two did is your business, but why did your neighbor tell us that Ramon was there?"

"I'm not saying anything else."

"Is that all you have to say about this matter?" Thompson asked.

"I've told you all I know."

"We'll be back. We're not done yet. I would ask you to stay in Borrego Springs for a few days, but that might be breath wasted." Thompson tipped his hat.

Lizzie watched them leave in a row of comically mismatched sizes and shapes. *There goes my relaxation and my tan*, she thought, fuming.

~

On the way back in the patrol car, Thompson lost no time making his opinion known.

"She's a piece of work, that one. I think it's clear as day. She had a thing with the other brother, so they popped Ramon and now Raoul's on the run with the money."

"I don't know," Henderson considered, "why would they have to get rid of Ramon if Raoul and Lizzie wanted to be together? Raoul's the one who's married, not Ramon."

"If they wanted to be together, they chose a very strange way to go about it," Ling agreed. "Considering Raoul's disappearance, the whole thing doesn't make any sense."

"How about the drug story with the peyote and mushrooms? What a bunch of baloney," Thompson continued, undeterred.

"The drug angle doesn't seem to fit with what we've learned about Ramon Matus," Ling said.

"What chills me to the bone are the drawings of heaps of funeral flowers I saw in Matus's studio," Henderson said.

They drove the rest of the way in silence, looking out at the desert plain, without a single flower in sight.

28

FRIDAY, DECEMBER 20, 4:30 P.M.

R aoul continued driving south. He'd started at 8:00 in the morning after leaving Lizzie's apartment and just kept going through the day, until the sun began to dip into the Pacific Ocean to his right.

He'd crossed the border road in his Toyota pickup truck and drove straight down Baja California. He'd breezed through Tijuana and picked up the toll road on to Ensenada. In Rosarito he passed the old Rosarito Beach Hotel with its faded charm and glamour. After Ensenada the road became narrower and he encountered fewer cars. The large billboards advertising condo developments became sparse. He drove past trash and plastic bags that had accumulated on both sides of the road because nobody bothered to pick them up.

He drove through drawn-out villages lining the road. They consisted of a long line of small shops and stands cobbled together with odd pieces of wood or metal. The stalls displayed colorful serapes and blankets, sombreros with gaudy hatbands, large glazed flowerpots for patios up north, stuffed figures of comic book heroes like Batman and Spider-Man, trinkets the store owners thought tourists would like to buy as souvenirs. Mostly they lingered on display, accumulating the dust of the road.

Raoul drove past *panaderías*, where he could have bought tasty *pan dulces*, sweet breads in the shape of conch shells, covered with a thick crust of brown sugar. He drove by small children squatting by the side of the road in their cheap flip-flops. He drove barely noticing any of this. He saw his surroundings, but they didn't register.

Raoul's thoughts were so turbulent and overwhelming they blocked out everything else. He didn't stop to eat or drink. Only when he reached the emptiness of the desert beyond Punta Colonet did he start to breathe deeply again.

No thoughts of his wife, his children, his parents, or his business had been able to penetrate the turmoil in his mind. Lizzie figured in his thoughts, but he doubted that she would become a permanent part of his life. What had he done?

So many emotions had been stirred up by the events of the last two days. Some feelings were like scrap metal scratching big cuts into the surface of his heart. Scraps he thought he'd buried many years ago now reemerged with unexpected force. How was he going to deal with all that debris? He had no idea, so he just kept driving.

Raoul finally stopped the car on a turnout in the road. He had a few water bottles in the cab for the long, hot hours he spent working on people's roofs. He drank some water and sat in the back of his truck on top of tarps he used to wrap tools or cover whatever he did not want to become sticky with tar. He watched the sunset over the Bahía San Ramón.

When he entered Lizzie's apartment in the hours before dawn, he had intended to comfort her. She'd cried on his shoulder and he'd held her. They drank two glasses of whiskey to get over their shock and the grief. Lizzie leaned into him and her hair tickled his cheek like small live wires sending tiny pleasurable shock waves through his skin. All he remembered was the smell of her hair and the softness of her face as he touched her lips and the lids of her closed eyes. They'd gotten carried away in the drama of the moment.

How could he have done this to his wife and brother?

~

A scene from his childhood emerged in his mind. His brother Ramon was about fifteen years old. Raoul had been ten. Ramon stood over José Hernandez in the schoolyard after giving him a good thrashing. José was the bully who had tormented Raoul for months. He had called Raoul a rat and a dirty Indian, a person even the Mexicans didn't want. Then José ambushed him on his way home armed with sticks and stones. He bombarded Raoul until he had to shield his head and run for cover into one of the little grocery stores in the barrio. The store owners had no sympathy for him and told him to get lost unless he bought something.

At the time, Ramon was already in high school. Ramon was not afraid or ashamed to be an Indian. He proudly wore his hair long, and when he found out about the bullying, he gave José a good beating. Ramon was strong and a lot taller than Raoul and his classmates, who he remembered standing in a semicircle in the schoolyard around José on the ground. They faced off against Ramon, who seemed almost relaxed, but ready to strike again should anybody as much as lift a finger.

Raoul stood behind his brother, feeling small and proud. Ramon radiated a dark temper, a force you did not want to mess with. Nobody said a word. Ramon looked each of Raoul's classmates in the eye, one after the other. He took his time, calmly, not threatening, but his gaze lingered on their faces as if to memorize their features. José was still on the ground between them, not hurt badly, except in his pride; caught up in the moment like everybody else, he was unable to move. So he just stayed down there in the dust.

Ramon finished the inspection of all the frozen faces. "Go," he said calmly, and as if released from a spell, they all scrambled to life. José got up first and ran off.

On their way home, the brothers didn't need to say anything to each other, nor did they ever mention the encounter to their parents. Raoul never had a problem with the bullies again.

Everybody at school respected Ramon, even the teachers. Not that he tried to fulfill their expectations. He didn't need to. Ramon was simply himself. Unlike Raoul, who tried to please everybody: his teachers, his parents, his wife, his children, his clients, his neighbors, the state, society . . . Though he never had to please Ramon. Ramon had never needed him, but he had accepted and loved him.

The more Ramon withdrew into his stillness, and the less he needed anybody, the more people offered him their affection. Teachers wrote him letters of recommendation, for college, for scholarships, which he accepted gracefully, but not gratefully. He hadn't asked for them, after all.

At this point in his stream of thoughts, Raoul broke down sobbing on his truck bed. His proud, powerful, invincible brother was dead. Raoul had had to work hard for every little achievement. He'd had to work for his grades, his exams, for every bit of praise and acknowledgement his parents and teachers cared to spoon out to him. Why was he the one who survived?

The sun had dipped into the ocean in a splash of gaudy colors. Raoul was getting cold, and he wrapped himself in the blankets and crawled back into the cab of the truck. He curled up on the seat. It felt good to be out here alone, not stifled in his small bedroom. The night was black and it would be long. It was the night before winter solstice, he remembered. It felt right to be out here in the Mexican desert on the longest night of the year. He had to keep going on this road a while longer, before he could return and face his family. Before falling asleep, he thought, Ramon would have approved.

29

SATURDAY, DECEMBER 21, 9:00 A.M.

J erome: Two men and five women sat in a circle on the floor of La Casa Del Zorro's bright conference room.

"Welcome to the Winter Solstice Retreat," began Jerome Schlesinger. "As you know, the winter solstice is a very special time of the year. Maybe even the *most* special time. The longest night of the year may not mean that much to us today. We light up our darkness with electric bulbs in all colors and fill the silence of the night with TV, iPods, and other electronic devices. The longest night of the year used to be the coldest, darkest, and most hopeless night, especially in northern regions. The night farthest away from warmth, abundance, food, green trees, plants, and blue skies."

Jerome looked around the room at the faces turned toward him. He had their attention.

"It doesn't have the same meaning of scarcity and deprivation for us anymore. Actually, most of us eat too much during the holidays, not too little. But the longest night also symbolizes a time of spiritual emptiness, when we feel far away from our inner warmth and light. That's why we're here. That's why our pagan ancestors invented the tree of light long before Christianity adopted it. The longest night can only be followed by the second shortest day. The beginning of longer days and earlier dawns. The reemergence of light after a long darkness. The beginning of hope, at the lowest point. That's what we are here to celebrate and experience."

Jerome saw a flicker of interest in the face of the French man with the chipped tooth. Good; even if he could reach just one person, his effort was worth it.

"You have come here to the desert, where the nights are still dark and the stars are still visible. I congratulate you on that choice. Now that you are here, for whatever reasons, please try to really be here; be present. I realize that you have come from different directions, from different lives, different circumstances, different jobs, families, conflicts. Of course you carry all that with you into the retreat, and it can be fruitful for your practice."

He paused to let his last words sink in; to allow them time to arrive here in this moment.

"So let's begin with Spiritual Law Five: *Slow down your pace, until you can hear your own thoughts.* Some of those thoughts may not be pleasant. Remember, this is the longest night. We may have a hard time hearing our thoughts. We may have a hard time slowing down. We may be so used to running an inner monologue, the chatter going on in our minds, that we don't even hear it anymore, like the background music in an elevator. Let's take a few deep breaths and listen to ourselves. You don't have to tell me or anybody else what those thoughts are; just be aware of them, whether they are positive or negative or just confused.

Spiritual Law Three states: *Don't avoid uncomfortable feelings and thoughts and seek out the pleasant ones. Observe, investigate, and experience them fully.* Welcome your thoughts and feelings like guests; look at them and then let them go again, slowly."

Jerome paused. He went on to tell the group the story of his preparation the previous day. As planned, he wove in Spiritual Law #1: *Act, don't react,* and Law #8: *Be in the moment. It will never come back and it is the only one you've got.* Then he gave them each a few moments.

"Close your eyes and take a few deep, slow breaths. Acknowledge the arising thoughts, without either suppressing or holding onto them.

Slow down your pace. You are in a peaceful, safe place, in the beautiful desert. All you have to do is arrive, here and now."

~

Lizzie: After she had closed her eyes and sat in silence, Lizzie's thoughts darted around her head like birds in a cage. She immediately felt fidgety and questioned her decision to come to this retreat. She could barely remember why she was here. She heard Jerome's voice urging calmly:

"Take a deep, slow breath and listen to your thoughts. Don't judge them or yourself, just look at them and acknowledge them."

Lizzie took a deep breath. Okay, she was here because Ramon had a letter from this man in his pocket when he died. Did that really mean anything? Was that more than pure coincidence? Did that justify her being here? Ramon had not sought out this self-help guru, rather the other way around. There was a connection between the two, and that's why she was here, because that was all she had left of Ramon. The last connection, except of course his brother . . . but she did not want to think about him right now. Jerome's voice softly penetrated her mind.

"Allow your thoughts to unfold, the uncomfortable ones as well as the pleasant ones. Don't edit, don't override. Let them come and go in your mind, and they will lose their power over you."

All right, she'd let the thoughts about Raoul emerge. They weren't that threatening anyway. He was a nice, kind man, who happened to look a lot like Ramon. He had been there when she was sad and upset and outraged that Ramon was gone. He had been a momentary substitute. It had been a comfort for both of them. No harm done. It wouldn't happen again.

Too bad that old hag Shmelkes had seen him and told the police. What an ugly drag she was. Lizzie might have to look for another apartment to get rid of her, or else find some other way to shut her up. Still, it wasn't the end of the world. She'd get over it, and nobody had done anything criminal.

That thought brought her to the question of Ramon's $20,000 withdrawal. She had to talk to her dad about that. It didn't feel right.

Ramon had been very frugal. He never spent much on himself. What had he intended to do with the money? It was very puzzling and confusing.

"Where are you now? Let the thoughts go like clouds in a blue desert sky. Arrive, here and now!" Jerome's voice came from far away.

She was here in the Anza-Borrego Desert, a place Jerome Schlesinger called safe, beautiful, and peaceful, and yet a very ugly crime had taken place here only three days ago. She wanted to go into the desert where the murder had taken place, the dark and dangerous place. She had no real interest in this nice and harmless space. She needed to understand the mystery, the hatred, the violence. That's why she was here.

Lizzie opened her eyes and saw the speckled sunlight spread on the white floor like the lace of a wedding dress. Despite herself, she had to admit it looked beautiful.

Vega: "Close your eyes and take a few deep, slow breaths. Acknowledge the arising thoughts, without either suppressing or holding onto them. Slow down your pace. You are in a peaceful, safe place, in the beautiful desert. All you have to do is arrive, here and now," said Jerome's voice.

Vega closed her eyes. She'd had a head start because she'd already spent a couple of days at La Casa Del Zorro. She felt the warmth of the sun on her back and heard the gurgling fountain in front of the open windows. It was all so idyllic and peaceful, if she could only stop thinking and be in the moment, as Schlesinger suggested.

Her thoughts took on some urgency. After the conversation with Deputy Ling in the Fox Bistro, Vega realized she was a person of interest in the murder case. There were too many connections.

There was only one explanation for Schlesinger's letter in Ramon's pocket: Ramon had been on his way to La Casa Del Zorro to meet with Jerome. How did he know Jerome was here? Could Jerome have helped him? Did Ramon need help? Did they meet? Or did he have an appointment of a different kind? It made Vega anxious to think there might be a killer in this desert where her sons and husband were out hiking at this very moment.

"Take a deep, slow breath and listen to your thoughts. Don't judge them or yourself, just look at them and acknowledge them," Vega heard Jerome say.

She took a deep breath and tried to let the anxiety go. She had a bad feeling, and just hoped her sons and Greg were safe.

Vega wondered if there was a clue in Ramon's work that could explain his murder. Had he created powerful enemies? Ramon's work implied a criticism of cross-border policies by sympathizing with the illegal migrants crossing the border, risking their lives. But it was such a subtle criticism and such a vague, amorphous entity to accuse, more like a flaw of the system and society. She could not imagine anybody taking personal offense. Unless it was a "coyote" worried about his human trafficking business. Maybe Ramon had interfered with some of the ruthless human smugglers while trying to help their illegal clients. Vega's thoughts were running away with her now, as she imagined the fateful encounter in the desert at night.

"Allow your thoughts to unfold, the uncomfortable ones as well as the pleasant ones. Don't edit, don't override. Let them come and go in your mind, and they will lose their power over you," Jerome prompted.

She had only known Ramon superficially, but she knew his work, which was anything but superficial. She remembered a passage from the exhibition catalogue she had written after interviewing Ramon in his studio. *In his installation* Darkness *the visitor enters a completely black space. Only after a few minutes, several faintly glowing shapes and stones emerge and provide guidance and orientation, as well as a way out. Like this installation, Ramon Matus deserves a second glance, a few moments of contemplation to allow some of the deeper layers of his work to emerge.*

Maybe there was something to her theory. Maybe she should talk to the police about it. She knew Ramon's work deeply. She needed to visualize his installations and let them guide her, just like the faintly fluorescent rocks in his *Darkness* installation led the viewer out of the black room.

In her mind she pictured another one of his pieces. It was a giant

boulder with jagged edges. Installed in a gallery with the right light-
ing, the heavy rock cast a sharp shadow on the floor. But the shadow of
the boulder was not black. Matus had filled it with a multitude of
colors and images, a kaleidoscope of impressions, patterns, and images
of the desert and the night sky, all filling the shape of the shadow,
moving, merging, morphing. They were emitted from an invisible
projector on the ceiling. It was a fascinating work of art. In order to
figure out what had happened to Ramon, she needed to understand:
What shadow did Ramon's death cast?

"Where are you now? Let the thoughts go like clouds in a blue
desert sky. Arrive, here and now!"

Vega felt as though she had been on the verge of discovering something important, but now it had vanished like the traces of a dream.
Obediently, she opened her eyes and let the thought go.

Betsy closed her eyes hesitantly. Her eyelids fluttered. She did not
really want to shut them. She was a wide-eyed kind of person. Betsy
would have preferred to talk to someone, anyone, such as the friendly-
looking blond woman sitting next to her in the circle. She really
wanted to meet all the other participants. Maybe she should suggest
that Mr. Schlesinger, who seemed like a very fine gentleman, go
around and ask everybody to introduce themselves. She glanced
around and thought that each person looked very interesting. But they
all had their eyes closed. Except Mr. Schlesinger's wife, who now
winked at her, and the other man in the room, the one with the
chipped tooth. His face looked like a contorted mask. Whatever went
through his mind was neither peaceful nor relaxing. He looked terrified. *Poor man, I don't want to know what you are thinking*, Betsy thought.
She smiled at him and he closed his eyes. Reluctantly, Betsy closed her
eyes too.

"Take a few deep, slow breaths. Acknowledge the arising thoughts,
without either suppressing or holding onto them. Slow down your
pace," she heard Schlesinger say.

I really don't know what thoughts he is talking about, thought Betsy.

"You are in a peaceful, safe place, in the beautiful desert. All you have to do is arrive, here and now," he continued.

It is really very beautiful and peaceful here, Betsy thought. Betsy had not seen a single brown or wilted rose blossom. This morning she had taken an early walk around the premises and found the groundskeepers raking and grooming the flowerbeds. They'd greeted her, smiling and friendly. They were Mexican, like her cleaning woman, Josefina. They removed every brown or yellow leaf from the rosebushes carefully, and the roses looked so beautiful and fresh, with little dewdrops balancing like pearls on their petals. There were pink, white, red, yellow, and orange-streaked rose blossoms. Each had a different scent. Betsy knew how much care it took to feed and trim those bushes. She had some on her patio, but they did not look half as good as the roses here. When the gardener in his smart Casa Del Zorro uniform realized how much the roses delighted her, he had clipped a perfect yellow one and given it to her. What a charming, lovely man! It was now on her bedside table in a water glass in her tasteful guestroom, with its own little fireplace and view of the pool.

Betsy relished the thought of the crisp, white bedsheets and the marble shower. After her morning walk, she'd had a phenomenal breakfast with fresh-squeezed grapefruit juice and a bread basket filled with oven-fresh croissants and muffins. If only her husband could be here to share all this delight. But her husband was at a conference. Betsy did not want to be alone just days before the holidays, so she had decided to come to this retreat. Her husband had read Schlesinger's book and thought it was a good idea, and the photos of the desert resort had looked so enticing. Betsy thought it might help her become more calm and serene, even though her husband claimed there was no chance of that. She thought serenity would suit her, but now that she was here, she really had no idea what she was supposed to be thinking about.

"Take a deep, slow breath and listen to your thoughts. Don't judge them or yourself, just look at them and acknowledge them," Schlesinger's voice floated into her consciousness.

Betsy took a deep and relieved breath. Apparently it was not a problem that she did not know what to think about. Whatever came up was okay. Suddenly her cleaning woman, Josefina, came to her mind. *Isn't that something*, she thought. Where had the thought come from? Maybe the Mexican gardeners had reminded her. Since Mr. Schlesinger had told her to let the thoughts arise, Betsy allowed them to linger on Josefina. She was such a great help to her and a good and thorough cleaner, even if she was a bit clumsy. And very reliable, except for last Thursday. Josefina's daughter-in-law, Tina, had called and explained that there was a death in the family. Josefina's son. How devastating!

Betsy did not have any children of her own, but she was fond of kids and she imagined it must be the worst nightmare for any mother to lose her child. Betsy would have to do something very nice for Josefina, something super nice like . . . She could not think of anything nice enough to give comfort for losing one's son. She always gave Josefina nice lunch trays, but that was nothing special. She could buy her a gift, definitely flowers, and maybe a nice cashmere shawl, warm and soft, for the holidays. But as Betsy pictured giving Josefina the shawl, she suddenly realized it was an awfully inappropriate and inadequate gift for losing a son. It was almost an insult, belittling the scale of Josefina's loss. No, Betsy would only be showing her utter ignorance of what it meant to lose a child. But what was she going to do instead?

She felt entirely at a loss and very helpless, something that rarely happened. Most of the time, she knew how to please people, and it gave her pleasure to dispense food and gifts. But this situation was beyond her scope of experience, beyond the emotions of her sheltered life. She felt sad and poorly equipped to deal with this problem. She was close to tears. Betsy tried to fight back the tears and get a hold on her emotions, when she heard Schlesinger say, "Allow your thoughts to unfold, the uncomfortable ones as well as the pleasant ones. Don't edit, don't override. Let them come and go in your mind, and they will lose their power over you."

Betsy took a deep breath and let the sadness wash over her. Tears ran down her cheeks and she let them flow without worrying about her makeup. It felt like a relief to let the tears run freely. There was just no way around it: losing your child was an irreparable tragedy and nothing could alleviate that. There was no way to make it better or less painful. It was just unbearably tragic, and for a moment Betsy felt at one with Josefina, shared that pain for one second, and that was maybe the greatest gift of all. She felt cleansed and somewhat calmer.

"Where are you now?" Jerome's voice asked gently. "Let the thoughts go like clouds in a blue desert sky. Arrive, here and now!"

Betsy opened her eyes and wiped the tears away with the sleeves of her new white cotton shirt. No sweat suit for her, nothing so vulgar. The crisp white blouse was paired with freshly starched and pressed jeans. They were a bit uncomfortable for sitting on the floor cross-legged, but she had a few pillows to prop her up and there was no force in the world that could make her wear sweatpants. The mere sound of the word was disgusting and made her want to hold her nose. Her freshly laundered shirtsleeves showed makeup stains from her mascara, where she had wiped her eyes. Betsy smiled. It didn't matter; she didn't really care.

Hilde sat with her eyes almost closed. Jerome had done a good job with the introduction. Of course, she had heard it many times before. She blinked carefully at the other participants. The little lady with the blond bangs in the white blouse and jeans stared back at her with wide-open eyes. Hilde winked at her. She obviously had a hard time relaxing and concentrating. Hilde could relate to that. She'd much rather be out in the lobby, finishing the books, processing the final payments, and seeing to it that lunch was ready on time. There was just too much to do. But as the wife of the author of *The Ten Laws of Spiritual, Mental, and Emotional Expansion*, she had to show solidarity. She had to set an example by following his prompts and validating his teaching.

Of course, she was his first and most ardent fan. Actually, she saw herself more as his business manager, because that's what he really needed and what she was good at. He had enough followers, but he was hopeless with numbers, and money, and keeping the books. He was just too removed and deeply engrossed in his philosophical thoughts. That was fine with Hilde. That's what she loved about him. They complemented each other.

Maybe if Betsy, as she now recalled the name of the little lady in the white blouse, would finally close her eyes, then Hilde could slip out and finish her paperwork. She still had to respond to three media requests. Jerome was reluctant to do so many interviews, but the publicity was a windfall for them. They'd almost had to cancel this retreat for lack of participants (of course, she had not told Jerome how bad it was). Fortunately, they got those last two registrations as a result of the media coverage, or if you wanted to be a stickler about it, as a result of Ramon Matus's death.

A very tragic event. She had not known the man, but apparently Jerome had thought highly of him. They should hold this retreat in Matus's memory and honor. What a brilliant idea. The media would love it. She had to tell Jerome as soon as this meditation was over.

"Close your eyes and take a few deep, slow breaths. Acknowledge the arising thoughts, without either suppressing or holding onto them. Slow down your pace."

Hilde sighed. Slowing down was the hard part for her. She liked to be on the go, playing tennis, doing errands. It seemed a bit tedious and unproductive to just sit there. Of course, she would never admit that to her husband or anybody else, because slowing down was so important to him. It was a good thing he had her. Since she was so much younger, she could do all the things that required speed and action. She drove him around and set up his seminars and appointments. They were a good team.

"Take a deep, slow breath and listen to your thoughts. Don't judge them or yourself, just look at them and acknowledge them."

He'd just said it. She did not have to feel bad for not liking these meditations. Hilde blinked again. Oh good, Betsy had finally closed her eyes. They were all in relaxation mode, doing their internal observations. She just had to slip out noiselessly.

Oh no, Betsy was crying now! Hopefully this wasn't going to turn into an emotional breakdown. It wouldn't be the first time. Hilde knew how to deal with them, but she'd prefer it didn't happen right at the beginning of the first day. Breakdowns always had a very unsettling effect on the rest of the participants. This development meant she couldn't leave. She had to keep an eye on Betsy.

If only Jerome wouldn't encourage them to give in to their emotions so much. Hilde saw no use in that. In her opinion, you kept a grip on yourself, stayed in control. Jerome did not understand that. He was so emotional and sensitive. Hilde loved that about him, but she was sure he had no idea how much work it took to protect him and enable him to give in to his feelings. Without her, he'd be lost. He wouldn't even know what to wear. He couldn't even access their bank account.

"Allow your thoughts to unfold, the uncomfortable ones as well as the pleasant ones. Don't edit, don't override. Let them come and go in your mind, and they will lose their power over you."

Well, she'd had just about enough unfolding thoughts for today. She needed to actually get some work done. But Hilde didn't want to complain. Jerome and she had a good, comfortable, even luxurious life. She made sure of that. Jerome needed her, and she couldn't do it without him. She'd never be able to write a book or give seminars and speeches. He was so much wiser and deeper. Just a bit helpless as well. People would take advantage of him without her. Thanks to his books and her money management skills, they had a beautiful house overlooking a river valley and they spent time in luxurious resorts such as this one . . .

"Where are you now? Let the thoughts go like clouds in a blue desert sky. Arrive, here and now!"

I am here, dear, Hilde thought. *I arrived exactly on time.*

Bertrand did not want to close his eyes. He tried to stay awake as much as possible, because whenever he closed his eyes the terror began. He had come to this retreat for distraction, to focus his mind on something other than himself, and now the instructor threw him back into his own misery. Should he just get up and leave? He had paid good money for this retreat. Bertrand looked around. Would anybody even notice if he slipped out? The little blond lady in the white blouse looked him straight in the eyes and smiled. The instructor's wife squinted at him. He would give it a few more minutes, not more.

"Take a deep, slow breath and listen to your thoughts. Don't judge them or yourself, just look at them and acknowledge them."

Easy for you to say, thought Bertrand. *You probably have nothing worse to think about than your next book or seminar.* As soon as Bertrand closed his eyes, the usual images predictably flooded his mind: the boardinghouse in Marseille, the shabby staircase, the noise and the stale smell of beer from the bar on the ground floor, the green wallpaper. Bertrand tried to stop here, but the images kept coming, like a movie on a loop, repeating themselves over and over again. He had to continue to walk behind the drab kitchen counter, even though he already knew what awaited him there: the dead body of Nicole, swimming in her own blood, killed by one of his own kitchen knives.

She still wore her black stockings and the green dress. She would wear those clothes for all eternity. Just like her image on the grimy linoleum floor would always stay the same in his mind. Unable to stop the sequence, he put a cigarette into her dead hands. There was nothing more he could do for her. Nicole had been his love and his curse. She had also been the lover of Maurice, crime boss of the French Connection, before she came to Bertrand. By then she had already ruined Bertrand's life, his career, and his future.

Nicole had seemed so alluring and promising when he first saw her as a young chef at the restaurant Pied au Cochon in Strasbourg. Now she lay dead before him. After putting the last cigarette into her hand, he'd fled from the safe house in Marseille. Maurice and his gang had chased him out of Strasbourg, after he testified against them. Now the French police were after him as well. The dead body of Maurice's lover lay in the apartment witness protection had provided for him. Now he was a witness on the run. He'd fled across the Atlantic and across the entire American continent until he reached this small desert town, surrounded by mountains and protected by endless stretches of sand and badlands. He'd stopped running because the people here did not care where he came from as long as he kept pouring their drinks. He'd stopped here because he thought he was safe, but the images and the nightmares came after him. They caught up with his dreams and every idle waking hour.

"Allow your thoughts to unfold, the uncomfortable ones as well as the pleasant ones. Don't edit, don't override. Let them come and go in your mind, and they will lose their power over you."

It would be such a relief if the thoughts and images lost their power and left him in peace for a while, but how many times did he have to confront the same inner movies? At first it was just Nicole, but then there were other dead bodies he had seen.

It had not taken long before the Border Patrol took an interest in Bertrand. He was an outsider in Borrego Springs with a questionable past. He had his certificate from the culinary school in Strasbourg, but his immigration papers and work permits were sketchy. They'd made him an offer he could not refuse. Bertrand became a police informant in exchange for keeping his liquor license and a green card.

What sounded like a good deal at first went sour quickly. Those he was supposed to inform on, the cartel members, found him as well and made him a proposition he could refuse even less. Become a double agent, or lose your business and your right hand. Bertrand valued both and learned to play the game both ways. Once in a while he had to give the police something. He gave them small crooks, those the cartels grew tired of or wanted to get rid of anyway. He had made up the two men he told McInness about, but he knew he had to give him something. If necessary they could come up with two men fitting the description, and they would leave him alone for a while. But with all the media coverage, the police would not be satisfied with nothing. *It will get hot around here*, thought Bertrand. *Even in the middle of winter.*

"Where are you now? Let the thoughts go like clouds in a blue desert sky. Arrive, here and now!"

Where am I? thought Bertrand. *I'm on the run, as always. I'm between a rock and a hard place. I'm in purgatory. I'm trapped in a boardinghouse in Marseilles. I'm trying to evade the Sheriff and McInness and the cartel. I'm trying not to drink myself to death.*

Bertrand did not want to open his eyes.

~

Paula Patterson closed her eyes, just to be a team player. She was a journalist, not a participant in this retreat. She wanted to write about it, not experience it. In her mind, she considered the questions she wanted to ask Jerome Schlesinger. When had he started to meditate? What set him on his path as a self-help guru? Why had he given up his former professional career? Paula only knew that Schlesinger had been a media executive. How was his book supposed to help people in their professional and personal lives? And finally: What was his connection to Ramon Matus?

Paula heard Schlesinger's soothing voice.

". . . take a few deep, slow breaths. Acknowledge the arising thoughts, without either suppressing or holding onto them. Slow down your pace. You are in a peaceful, safe place, in the beautiful desert. All you have to do is arrive, here and now."

It was quite pleasant to sit here. She had her questions pretty much prepared. Maybe it was okay to relax for a few minutes. The space was quiet, calm, and warm. She felt the sun on her back and heard the gently gurgling water outside. Slowly, Paula felt the muscles in her neck relax. She allowed her shoulders, jaws, and eyes to soften.

"Take a deep, slow breath and listen to your thoughts. Don't judge them or yourself, just look at them and acknowledge them."

Paula took a deep breath and suddenly something unexpected happened. She stopped thinking. As if she had emptied her head with the last exhale, she felt her mind expanding into a quiet and unlimited space. It was a bit scary to be pulled into this interior space and Paula was not quite sure this was supposed to be happening. Just in case, she continued breathing deeply. With her next breath, a wave of warmth and golden light bubbled up from her heart and filled her with joy and giddiness. The orange wave expanded beyond the boundaries of her person and streamed into the room beyond. Paula imagined it reaching the person sitting next to her, like a wave of fragrant, warm air. She was tempted to open her eyes and peek at her neighbor, the little blond lady, but already the next mushroom bubble rose from her center and filled her chest, her neck, and her head with well-being. *Better not question what it is*, Paula thought, *it feels so good.*

She allowed the peaceful substance to fill every corner and crevice of her body, before she breathed it out and sent it into the room beyond.

"Allow your thoughts to unfold, the uncomfortable ones as well as the pleasant ones. Don't edit, don't override. Let them come and go in your mind, and they will lose their power over you."

These pleasant sensations bubbling up weren't thoughts; they were like a current surging up from a spring deep inside. Paula tried to follow that source farther and farther inward.

"Where are you now? Let the thoughts go like clouds in a blue desert sky. Arrive, here and now!" said Jerome.

Paula snapped awake, almost annoyed to be brought back to the present. She opened her eyes quickly, slightly embarrassed by what she had experienced.

30

SATURDAY, DECEMBER 21, 11:00 A.M.

Ronald Cantor sat in the small but ultramodern office in the back of his gallery. On the wall behind his desk hung a painting by John Baldessari entitled *Terms Most Useful in Describing Creative Works of Art* and one by Ed Ruscha named *Noise*. True to its name, it simply spelled out the word: *Noise*.

The phone rang and he picked it up.

"Detective Vincelli, I've been expecting your call. My daughter Lizzie has kept me updated on the developments in this most tragic case."

He paused, listening.

"I'm putting you on speaker phone, detective. . . . Yes, I knew Ramon Matus fairly well. I have represented his work for nearly five years now."

Cantor got up from his Eames chair and started to pace his office.

"Was Matus a successful artist?" Vincelli's voice asked.

Cantor paused for a moment. "Successful? I would say he was an *emerging* artist. His work was included in minor museum exhibitions. That always piques the interest of collectors and raises the value. But he was no art star. Not yet, anyway. He was still young; who knows where he could have gone, what he could have achieved . . . It's just very tragic."

"Do you have any of his work at the gallery right now?"

Cantor looked through the glass door of his office into the gallery space.

"We're showing a selection of his work. We had an opening yesterday, which was very well attended. I intend to expand the show with more work from Matus's studio and the private holdings of his family."

"Did anything sell?" Vincelli asked.

"We sold modestly, but it was respectable. Several collectors and one museum are considering buying one of his major installations."

"How unfortunate that Ramon Matus can't benefit from his success." Vincelli's voice sounded sarcastic.

"Indeed. Tragically, artists often become more successful in death than they were in life."

"Did Matus's work fetch prices above ten thousand dollars? Let's say twenty thousand?" Vincelli asked.

"Twenty thousand?" Cantor repeated and drummed a little rhythm on his desk with his fingers. He didn't like to talk about money over the phone. "None of his pieces fetched that much."

"Would he've had access to an amount of twenty thousand dollars?" Vincelli asked.

"If he lived frugally, like Lizzie tells me he did, then he could have saved up that much within the past two years or so."

A gallery assistant came into the office, and Cantor covered the mouthpiece and pushed the button to turn off the speaker phone.

"If you want to know more about his personal friends and habits, you'd better talk to Lizzie. I was his art dealer. I visited his studio, encouraged certain aspects of his work. I advised him, believed in him, but we didn't become close personal friends. I suppose for that I was too old, and too busy, and live too far away."

In response to Vincelli's next question, he said, "I only saw him about once every three months. And I didn't notice any changes in him recently. Again, Lizzie would know more about that."

After another pause, he said, "The desert was his stage, his arena.

He loved the desert, he worked there. I don't know whom he met there, but I am sure he had a good reason to be there."

Then, "Of course, Detective Vincelli, my pleasure. If you have any other questions please feel free to call me. It would be my pleasure to show you around the gallery and tell you all I know about Ramon Matus's work."

Finally, he said, "You have a great weekend as well, and happy holidays!"

Cantor still had the telephone receiver in his hand. He stared out into the gallery at Ramon's giant boulder, casting its colorful, moving shadow.

31

SATURDAY, DECEMBER 21, 12:00 NOON

A ll was not well in the Matus household. Josefina had gone to bed on Friday and did not want to get up in the morning. She complained of a headache, a stomachache, a backache, and fatigue. She had drawn her ruffled curtains and lay in the semidarkness, refusing to talk to anybody. There was still no word from Raoul. Marcos had to fill in for him in the roofing business, which was very hard on his old joints.

Tina tried to hold things together, but she felt close to tears most of the time. The Christmas decorations sat in boxes on the living room floor. Nobody had the time or inclination to buy a tree. The two boys, Jaime and Juan, were on Christmas vacation. Tina hadn't seen Jaime since yesterday, and Juan sat for hours between the boxes playing video games. The clashes and screams of his virtual warriors reached Tina in the kitchen at regular intervals.

"Where is your brother?" Tina called through the open door, trying to keep the panic under control.

"I don't know. Maybe he slept over at a friend's house," Juan answered indifferently.

"Without telling us?" Tina shouted back over the din.

Juan shrugged his shoulders. "We're off school; he doesn't have to get up early."

"Lunch is ready," Tina announced.

"Just a minute! I'm in the middle of a battle."

"Am I going to sit here and eat all by myself? I made guacamole and quesadillas," tempted Tina. These computer games her son played drove her crazy. There was always another battle to fight, another level to conquer. And that was more important than talking to his mother or coming to eat. Juan didn't even look up at her.

"What about Grandma, can't she join you?"

"Grandma is sick in bed and won't talk."

"Grandpa?"

"Working, finishing up a roofing job."

"When's Dad coming back?"

"I don't know."

"Are we going to have a Christmas tree?"

"I hope so."

"How about presents?"

"I don't know."

Suddenly, Tina couldn't stand shouting to her son from the kitchen anymore. The tasks ahead just seemed too overwhelming. She sat down at the kitchen table and sobbed.

"Mom, please don't cry," said Juan, standing in the doorway, hesitant to enter the kitchen.

"I'm sorry." Tina pulled a crumpled and used tissue from her apron and blew her nose.

"It's okay, Mom. I'm going to help you get a Christmas tree." Juan watched from the door.

That was as close as he got. Tina knew a crying mom wasn't something Juan was ready to deal with. She was supposed to be the one comforting him.

"Thanks, sweetheart," Tina sobbed.

"Just stop crying, okay?"

32

SATURDAY, DECEMBER 21, 12:00 NOON

Lunch was a delicious and civilized affair on the terrace of La Casa Del Zorro. It consisted of seared chicken sandwiches on freshly baked panini, rosemary roasted potatoes, and arugula salad with strawberries, locally grown grapefruit slices, and roasted almond slivers. At the long table overlooking the rose garden, Jerome sat next to Paula, who had placed a little tape recorder before them to record their interview. Hilde and Betsy chatted animatedly. They had discovered a shared passion for fashion and flowers. Bertrand went home for lunch, skipping the second part of the program. As a local, he did not need the orientation of the nature walk, and as a restaurant owner, he preferred to eat at his own premises and oversee the lunch there. Lizzie sat next to Vega, who introduced herself. Vega was still nervous about her family, who had not returned from their hike yet.

"Are you the Vega Stern who wrote the essay about Ramon?" Lizzie asked, surprised.

"Yes, I am. Have you read it? You must be one of about five people total, including his family and gallery owner," Vega laughed.

"It's very good. I actually gave it to a police detective to read yesterday, so now there are six people," Lizzie corrected her.

"What a terrible tragedy his death is. Did you know Ramon?" Vega speared a piece of juicy grapefruit and strawberry with her fork.

"I was his girlfriend, and I'm the daughter of his art dealer," Lizzie said quietly.

"Ronald Cantor's daughter?"

"I'm Liz Cantor."

"I'm so sorry for your loss. It must be terrible for you. What an incredible coincidence that you are here," exclaimed Vega.

"It's not a coincidence," admitted Lizzie. "I came here because Ramon had a letter from Jerome Schlesinger in his pocket when he died. I came here to find out why."

"I heard about the letter. I, or actually my son Stevie, found Ramon."

"So many connections!" Lizzie said, puzzled.

"I'm afraid the police think there are too many connections and that they can't all be coincidental. I'm apparently on their list of suspects."

"Me too. They interrogated me here yesterday. I was supposed to stay in San Diego. But I left anyway."

"They told me to stick around as well. We plan to stay here until after the retreat, but then I need to get home for Christmas with my family," Vega said. "My children are worried about the Christmas celebration. They want to be home, where we have our Christmas tree and where Santa Claus can find them. They're afraid it will be too hard to locate them and deliver presents in the desert."

"We wouldn't want to risk that," Lizzie laughed.

"Liz, do you have any idea why Ramon came here? Did he say anything to you? Did he plan to meet with Schlesinger?" Vega asked urgently.

"No, he just said something about celebrating the winter solstice. You know he was into cosmic happenings. I thought coming to this retreat would give me some insight."

"What did you think of this morning?" Vega asked.

"At first I thought it was a complete waste of time. I didn't want to do the meditation. But after I settled down a bit, I noticed my thoughts getting clearer," Lizzie admitted.

"Me too. I thought about Ramon a lot, and I came up with a theory," Vega confided.

"Let's hear it." Lizzie leaned toward Vega.

"I think Ramon came out here to do an installation for the winter solstice. Perhaps an earthwork, I don't know. Maybe he has drawings about it somewhere," Vega began.

"The only drawings I found in his studio were of piles of flowers. They looked like a funeral."

"A funeral?" Vega paused to give this some thought. "I thought about who could take offense at Ramon's work. Nobody came to mind. He was a proponent of immigrants' rights. What if he came out here to work and somehow got in the way of a coyote, a human trafficker? What if Ramon tried to stop him or protect the people he was trying to bring into the country? The coyote might have turned on him."

"It's possible. You should tell the police about your theory." Lizzie was not overly convinced.

"I will. They may have considered this already. The problem is we have no proof, no witnesses. Didn't Ramon usually work with others? Maybe his brother would know."

"Ramon's brother has been missing since yesterday morning." Lizzie didn't look happy admitting this fact.

"Who else could he have spoken to? Any friends? Colleagues? You know who he associated with." Vega wasn't giving up yet.

"I think he had some cousins in Ensenada," Lizzie said.

"Cousins?"

Hilde interrupted their conversation, standing at the head of the table with her clipboard.

"Ladies, we hope you enjoyed lunch. We're now going on our nature walk in the desert. It's an orientation to get our bearings. To be conscious of where we are, where the sun sets, where the moon rises. We meet in fifteen minutes by the tennis courts," she announced breezily.

Jerome Schlesinger added, "This walk is going to place us firmly in the here and now geographically and cosmically prepare us for tonight. This morning we arrived with our bodies. Now we have to arrive with our minds. We look forward to seeing you in a few minutes."

The little group scattered back to their rooms for a few minutes.

33

SATURDAY, DECEMBER 21, 2:30 P.M.

After lunch, Bertrand had three hours to himself. He walked to his small apartment on Palm Canyon Drive, just a few hundred yards from his restaurant. Even though the apartment was small, two bedrooms and a living room with an open kitchen, it had a nice view of the Laguna Mountains to the south.

Bertrand didn't like enclosed spaces. He preferred living on the second floor, a rarity in the Borrego Springs valley. Buildings tended to spread out horizontally, not vertically. Most people lived either in sprawling adobe houses or in trailers in the middle of parched plots of land.

Bertrand felt safer up high, which was probably an illusion; it hadn't helped his nighttime sleep lately. He didn't want or need much space; two rooms were plenty, and the small kitchen was rarely used since he mostly ate at the restaurant. Bertrand plopped down onto his double bed and stared at the ceiling.

This retreat was a big mistake. He had signed up to make it through the holidays without drinking and to keep the memories at bay, but actually it had made them worse. Images of Nicole haunted him: Nicole, the beautiful, seductive, dangerous woman who had ruined his life; Nicole, who had cast her spell on him when he saw her for the first time as a young chef working at a restaurant in Strasbourg; Nicole, who had looked like a cross between a mermaid and a siren, with her green eyes and chestnut hair.

If Nicole hadn't entered his life, he would be a respected, maybe even celebrated chef in a restaurant in Strasbourg, or possibly Lyon or even Paris. He would be able to cook with fresh ingredients grown in lush gardens for people who'd appreciate his food.

How often had he unraveled the past back to the time before he met Nicole and imagined his alternative life, the life that could have been! But he always ended up again in this shabby apartment, with the blank walls and the beige day blanket on the bed; in a small town, where most people had never heard of the Alsace, in the midst of a parched desert that produced little more than cactus flowers.

Bertrand still loved to cook, but what the locals really wanted was American fare: burgers, fries, and beer. In addition to the culinary deficiencies, he felt squeezed between the Border Patrol and the cartels. Often Bertrand wondered how he had survived so long. One wrong move and he, too, would end up in the Canyon Sin Nombre, or in jail.

Why had he clung on for so long, surviving against all odds in this hostile environment? Was it really worth it? It wasn't fair that he had to suffer for so many years just because of one innocent mistake. A mere brush on the cheek from Nicole, like a kiss you give to a child or an acquaintance you haven't seen for years.

Bertrand could still feel her chestnut hair tickling his skin. He could still feel the excitement and his racing heart as she whispered *"Merci"* into his ear outside the restaurant one night. He could still smell her smoky breath as she leaned in close to him for a short moment. One moment too long as it turned out, because her lover, Maurice, the organized crime boss, stormed out of the restaurant and beat the shit out of Bertrand until he lay in a heap on the ground, unable to move.

All that because Bertrand, or Claude as he was called then, had shown Nicole a little kindness, had brought her a drink, an ashtray, and a lighter, as she came outside to get some night air and a few moments' peace away from her brutal lover. Bertrand was still paying the price from this incident, which had shaped his life, or ruined it, whichever way you wanted to look at it.

The image of Nicole, forever lying in her blood, forever wearing her green dress, forever dead on his kitchen floor in Marseille, still haunted him every day. She had joined him there, after running away from Maurice. It hadn't ended well.

Why had he survived? Hunted by the police as well as the organized crime squads, he'd found a freight ship that took him on as a cook across the Atlantic. Once he was on the American continent, he just kept going until he ran out of space to run, here in the Anza-Borrego Desert. But he couldn't outrun his past and he couldn't outrun the memories. They always caught up with him. Now another dead body had become part of Bertrand's baggage. Would he be next? Bertrand knew enough about what was going on in this border region to cost him his life many times over. He looked at the clock next to his bed. It was almost 5:00; time to go back to the restaurant. He was glad to have something to do. He didn't want to think anymore.

34

SATURDAY, DECEMBER 21

Raoul woke up stiff and cold. He didn't know where he was, and groped around in the dark for clues. Then it dawned on him: he was in the cab of his truck and he was very hungry. He scrambled out of his car and stumbled down to the pebbly beach in the semidarkness. The high tide rose almost to the incline of the road. The full moon had drawn the water up onto the rock-sprinkled beach and cast glistening highlights on the rippling waves.

Raoul yawned and squinted at the sky, which stretched in front of him in a dirty smear of gray and ragged charcoal clouds. He took a deep breath and waited until the first pink fingers of the rising sun touched the clouds. The world was quiet and empty and peaceful. Raoul didn't understand why he felt compelled to keep on driving south. But he had to keep going.

The sky slowly cleared and brightened. By the time he reached the village of San Quintín, the winter sun rose over the peninsula. Raoul stopped at a *panadería* and bought warm pastries, which he devoured with weak, black coffee. San Quintín looked like any other Baja road-side village. Rows of shack and huts lined the road on each side, offering food, tires, and souvenirs. Trash and plastic bags dotted the dirt shoulder of the road. Better to keep on driving.

The road past San Quintín hugged the shore of the Pacific, which looked crisp and clean in the early morning light. Raoul saw the landscape outside the window as if for the first time. Yesterday he had not seen his surroundings. His thoughts had been so thick and overwhelming as to block out all perception of the beauty of nature.

After thirty-five miles the road turned inland toward El Rosario, the last major supply hub for expeditions into the dry interior of Baja California Sur. Cars loaded with boats and kayaks, tents, bicycles, and Jet Skis waited in a long line at El Rosario's gas station. They filled up large water containers and extra gas canisters for their long drive through the desert. Raoul filled his tank and bought water bottles and two bags of tortilla chips to keep himself going. As he stored his supplies on the passenger side of his cab, he asked himself: *What is my plan? Where am I going? Shouldn't I contact my family?*

He took out his phone and checked it. The battery was dead, and even if he was able to charge it there was probably no service down here. He wouldn't have known what to say to Tina or his father anyway.

Raoul could not even explain to himself where he was going. He only knew that he had to continue driving. Guilt, grief, and confusion propelled him forward. If he just kept on going, the fog would lift and he would be able to see his life with new eyes. Or so he hoped. On the pile of newspapers next to the cash register at the gas station, Raoul saw the date was December 21. He realized it was the winter solstice. This day belonged to his brother Ramon's memory.

Equipped with his few supplies, he followed the road away from the coast into the hills and desert of central Baja. Large saguaro cacti dotted the rocky hills like oversized sentinels. In the morning light, the hills of Cerro la Esmeralda looked like a dramatic and desolate backdrop in a theater. Raoul had to concentrate on the dips and turns in the narrow curvy road. By noon he reached Cataviña, a way station with not much more to show for itself than a few dilapidated buildings and a small hotel.

Raoul entered the cool lobby with its terra-cotta-tiled floor to get lunch. Like many hotels in Baja, it was built in the Spanish hacienda style. Through a glass door Raoul glimpsed a two-tiered fountain in a central courtyard, which was surrounded by shady, arched arcades. At the rustic cantina, he had a burrito and beer. He looked out at the desert studded with saguaros and sagebrush. It felt good to sit down in the cool shade of the stone building, and Raoul lingered a bit. He wasn't in a hurry. On the whitewashed walls, he noticed photos of colorful rock paintings that looked ancient. When he asked the waitress about them, she explained that pictographs, believed to be several thousand years old—she was a bit vague on the exact age—could be found in caves close by.

"Cataviña is famous for its petroglyphs. They depict supernovas, and solar eclipses and other cosmic events that happened thousands of years ago," she declared proudly. Raoul was impressed and asked for directions to the caves. It did not sound too complicated. What better way to celebrate winter solstice than in a cave full of paintings by the ancients, connecting man and the cosmos? Ramon would have approved.

Two hours later, Raoul climbed through a rock crevice and into the first of the painted caves. He sat down to calm his breathing and to allow his eyesight to adjust to the darkness inside after the glaring sun of the desert. The cave opened to the west. As he looked out over the tumble of rocks and scattered cacti below him, Raoul let the slight breeze cool his flushed face. Yes, this was a good place to stop, think, and look; to let the thoughts and emotions wash over him until they subsided; to think of Ramon, to mourn him, to ask for forgiveness.

Raoul sat with his legs dangling outside the cave opening, watching the sun slowly sink behind the rocks in the west. As hour after hour passed, he began to feel the earth turning instead of the sun dipping. He began to see himself as a small speck in the turning wheels of the universe.

Before the light faded, he studied the cave paintings. Rust, charcoal, yellow, and white shapes covered the rock walls above him. There were concentric circles, circles with multicolored radiating rays, zigzag lines, triangles, squares with crosses, spirals, ladder shapes of parallel and connecting lines, amorphous shapes filled with dots. Raoul thought about these shapes. At first glance they looked like something his sons might have drawn in kindergarten. But the ancient artists had tried to capture what they observed in the sky above. They wanted to condense it and record it on the walls of this cave. Sitting within the ancient graffiti felt comforting to Raoul. His ancestors had tried to make sense of the mind-boggling variety of phenomena around them. Raoul could relate to that. They had tried to capture the patterns to better understand what was happening above. He was trying to make sense of his life and understand the pattern of what was happening to him.

The sun was barely above the mountain ridge in front of Raoul, ready to make its earliest departure of the year. A few orange rays cleared the rocky edge and extended to Raoul's position. They pierced his eyes, almost blinding him. To avert his gaze, he turned his head and he saw the last rays of the winter solstice sun light up the central image in the cave like a torch catching fire: a large yellow circle, surrounded by an orange ring with radiating yellow and charcoal lines, was illuminated by a perfectly centered spotlight of flaming rays from the setting sun. A living message sent over the centuries from his ancient ancestors to Raoul, who was here at the exact moment of the right day. They had created a cosmically aligned spotlight on the powerful image of the sun, which could only be seen on this one, special day of the year.

The last traces of warmth of the dying day touched Raoul's skin, and he felt physically connected to the cosmic drama of the longest night. For the first time in his life, he sensed that he really belonged here. Finally, he was at the right place in the right time in rhythm with the stars, the seasons, and the movement of the planets. A wave of gratitude washed over him. How lucky he was to be a part of this great pattern! At last he had been able to listen to his own voice and keep his appointment with the larger design of his life.

He knew his brother had felt the connection most of his life. What the ancient cave painters had created here, Ramon did with the tools and symbols of the twenty-first century. Ramon made the hidden patterns in people's lives visible through his art. It was so clear and so simple. How could he have missed it all these years?

The stars were here every night, but he had rarely seen them. The moon rose and made its journey across the sky but he had barely ever noticed it. The smells of the night, the whisper of the sagebrush's silver leaves, the scurrying of the mice—he had never really heard it, never smelled it before.

The sharp cold of the desert night crawled up his spine, but Raoul welcomed it. It made him feel alive. He felt as if a curtain had been lifted and suddenly he saw the world around him, really saw it as it was. Not filtered through his own worries, his own doubts and feelings of inferiority, not clouded by resentment and fear and the confines of his family and the responsibilities he carried. Raoul was content with the rocks, the stars, the hard surface underneath him, and his own breath in the cold night air. This cave, this moment, this night, cold, hunger, tiredness and all, filled him with great happiness.

He must have nodded off for a few hours, but when the first tinges of dawn crawled up the horizon, Raoul was ready to go home.

35

SATURDAY, DECEMBER 21, 7:00 P.M.

Only three people sat at the dinner table with the six place mats in the Matus household. Raoul, Jaime, and Josefina were missing. Josefina had taken a bit of chicken soup earlier, but still refused to get up for dinner. There was still no word from either Raoul or Jaime. Tina had left frantic messages and texts on both their cell phones, without any results. She had called all of Jaime's friends and their parents, but nobody had seen him. If Jaime didn't come home soon, she would have to report a second missing person in her family.

For dinner Tina had made chicken tamales and green chili salsa, a labor-intensive dish that had kept her occupied all afternoon. Both Jaime and Raoul loved it, and maybe she had hoped to lure them home with the smell of their favorite food. But only Marcos, Juan, and Tina ate the steaming cornmeal pouches silently and absentmindedly.

"Where can Jaime be?" Tina asked for the seventh time. "Should we call the police now?"

"He didn't sleep in his bed last night," volunteered Juan.

"He's just out with friends. It's Saturday night and he's on Christmas holiday," Marcos said, trying to calm her down.

"He is only fourteen. Where could he go?"

"Maybe he's at a friend's house," suggested Juan.

"I already called all his friends and nobody has seen him."

"Maybe you don't know all his friends," said Juan.

"And what about Raoul? He has been gone two full days."

"I don't know about Raoul, but the police are looking for him. They will find him." Marcos didn't really have a lot of confidence in the police, but he wanted to reassure his daughter-in-law.

"But in what condition?" Tina cried.

"He must be very upset about his brother," Marcos said.

"We're all distressed," she wailed. "How can he leave us at a time like this, when we really need him?"

"Sometimes a man has to be by himself for a while. He will be back," said Marcos, more confidently than he felt.

"What about me? I'd like to be by myself sometimes. Don't women have that right?"

"Tina, please calm down. Nobody is helped if you get hysterical now. *Mira*, Juan is here. He needs you."

"I know. I'm just so worried!"

"Listen, tomorrow, Juan and I are going to get a good, strong Christmas tree and you can take some time for yourself. The tamales are delicious, by the way, aren't they, Juan?" Marcos winked at his grandson.

"Very delicious," he mumbled.

Tina tried to smile back at him, but just then the phone rang. She jumped up as if stung by a bee. News, she hoped and feared, about her husband or son.

"What?" Tina gestured to her father-in-law, wide-eyed, shocked, helpless. "Where? Why? I'll be right there." She hung up. Her face had lost all color. "Jaime is in the hospital."

"Why? Was he in an accident?" Marcos asked calmly.

"They said something about an overdose. I didn't really understand. I have to go there right away." Already Tina had taken off her apron and smoothed her hair. She walked around the room like a sleepwalker, picking up things, dropping them, looking for her shoes.

"Okay, Juan, we need your help now," Marcos said, talking slowly and steadily. "You need to stay here and take care of your grandmother while your mother and I go to see Jaime, okay? This is very important.

Don't leave your grandma alone, under any circumstances. We depend on you, okay?"

"Yes, Grandpa, don't worry—you can rely on me."

"Good. I knew we could." Marcos clasped Juan's shoulder, then he got up, put on his jacket, grabbed the car keys for his station wagon, and handed Tina her coat. She still wore flip-flops, but that didn't matter now. Obediently she followed Marcos outside, moving in slow motion as if underwater.

At the hospital emergency room they were greeted by chaos. Two ambulances arrived with flashing lights and sirens. One unloaded a gurney with an old woman on life support, the other carried a young guy with a gunshot wound. Marcos grasped Tina's arm hard and steered her through the door. Doctors and nurses ran back and forth, receiving the new arrivals.

It took them a while to find Jaime's doctor, who took them to the young patient. Jaime lay in a hospital bed behind a curtain. It sectioned off a small space barely big enough to hold his bed and one chair. Jaime was unconscious. His face looked ashen, and he had an IV in his arm and a tube in his nose. He wore nothing but a diaper. Tina reeled.

"It looks worse than it is," the doctor explained pragmatically, talking fast and standing with one foot outside the cubicle. He clearly didn't have much time to spend on this case. "He has severe alcohol poisoning, probably mixed with prescription drugs. Kids get drunk and take pills simultaneously. They have no idea of the effect. How old is he?"

"Fourteen," said Tina.

"That's pretty young. He was lucky. He fell or was dragged to the little deli on Logan Avenue. A passerby called the ambulance."

"Who was with him?" Marcos asked.

"Nobody. Whoever he drank with left."

"How did you know to call us?"

"They left a note with his name and number. I still have it, if you want it."

"Yes, I'd like to see the handwriting."

"They're kids. We see this every day. He's going to be all right; he just has to stay here for the night until he sobers up enough to walk. He'll be out cold for a few hours."

"Why does he have all that tubing in him?"

"So he doesn't choke on his own vomit. We had to cut his clothes off; they were ruined."

As if on cue, Jaime started to gag and the doctor placed a kidney-shaped tray under his mouth.

"Thank you," Tina whispered. "I'm so embarrassed."

"*He* should be embarrassed. He could have died. His alcohol level was four times the legal limit. Has he done anything like this before?"

"No, never. And he will never do it again," Marcos said grimly.

"You need to talk to him. He probably had no idea about the damage he could cause. These kids are young and stupid, but a little parental intervention is in order here." The doctor looked at Tina and Marcos questioningly, as if wondering whether this was the mother with a much older husband.

"Don't worry. His life will change after tonight," promised Marcos. Tina started to cry. She sat down on the plastic chair.

"We can put another chair in here, if you want to wait until he wakes up," the young doctor offered. "And I need you to sign here, taking the financial responsibility for the ambulance and treatment here."

"How much is that going to be?" asked Tina, terrified.

"Probably a couple thousand dollars. Do you have insurance?"

"No, but we'll take care of it," assured Marcos, and he signed the form.

"Okay, then, I'll leave you with him. A nurse will check in on him periodically." He left quickly.

Marcos got another chair, and they sat down and stared at Jaime in silence.

"How are we going to pay two thousand dollars?" Tina asked in a timid voice.

"We'll figure it out."

"At least we found him," Tina said. "And he's going to be okay."

"Yes, he was lucky," agreed Marcos.

"What got into him? Drinking himself unconscious at fourteen?"

"We'll find out," promised Marcos.

"What're you going to do with him?"

"He's going to get a thrashing."

"Oh, I wish Raoul were here," Tina wailed.

"He would do the same thing," Marcos assured her.

"Did you do that to them when your boys were young?"

"You bet I did. How else are they going to learn what's right and wrong?"

"But Jaime is so young."

"That's the problem."

"Did Raoul get into trouble like this, when he was young?"

"I don't really remember. Maybe once or twice he got really drunk, but he was older and he was never in the hospital. Ramon never got drunk. He was always in control of himself. I told both boys what I'm going to tell Jaime: 'You are a Yaqui Indian; be proud of your heritage and don't bring shame on your tribe. There are already enough drunken Indians; don't become another one.'"

"Just a week ago, everything seemed fine. Now look at our family. It's falling apart."

"Our family has done well so far, and we'll recover again. We need to be strong."

"I know. I'm trying."

They sat silently, staring at Jaime and at the wall behind him. Tina found herself reading the bilingual label on the base of the bed over and over again. "When stationary always apply brakes." There was a green arrow pointing downward and a lever to push down to apply the brake. A red arrow pointed up. The two arrows danced around in Tina's mind like a yo-yo. She couldn't stop looking at the brake and reading the label, like a record with a scratch repeating the same groove over and over again. A nurse came in and asked if they wanted coffee. Both gratefully accepted.

Sipping the black and tepid coffee, Tina thought of Jaime as a young boy. She remembered when he was just four years old on the swing in their backyard. He kicked his feet as high as he could, his cheeks flushed and his black hair flying.

"Mom, look, I can touch the sky!" he would call.

"Jaime was a happy child," she said. "What went wrong? How did I not see this coming? Where have I failed as a mother and as a wife?" She looked at Marcos beside her. She only saw his profile, which was motionless and inscrutable. Where did he get the strength? He had just lost his son, his second son was missing, his wife was sick and depressed, his grandson was unconscious in the hospital, and now he had to deal with his hysterical daughter-in-law.

"Marcos, thank you for being here with me. I don't know what I'd do without you."

"It'll be all right, Tina. You'll see."

36

SATURDAY, DECEMBER 21, 7:30 P.M.

L izzie had been bored out of her mind during the nature walk. Too much talking, and not enough walking. All the other participants walked really slowly, plus there was basically nothing to see. It was desert, *duh*. After the walk everybody was on their own for dinner and the "big cosmic" event, so Lizzie went to the Fox Bistro for happy hour.

A good-looking young bartender, whose name tag identified him as "William, Jamaica"—all Casa Del Zorro employees wore name tags including their place of origin—served her a fabulous-looking frozen strawberry margarita garnished with a mini-umbrella. Lizzie smiled. The young Jamaican smiled back.

"Say, William," Lizzie began. "Where would you go in this town on a Saturday night?"

His face immediately turned very serious.

"That is a difficult question. I work most Saturday nights. We have live music and good food right here in the lounge if you don't want to go to the formal restaurant next door."

"William, listen, there must be people under the age of sixty in Borrego Springs and they must go somewhere on Saturday nights. You live here, don't you?"

"Yes, ma'am, for another fourteen months until my training is completed."

"Good, then tell me, where do you go on your night off?" Lizzie shook her hair back with a swirl.

"There is Bertrand's, but it's not as high class as here. The food's good and there is a bar."

"I already know about Bertrand's."

"Then there is Bill's Desert Rose Café, but I would not recommend it to a lady like yourself," William explained with emphasis.

"And why not?" Lizzie challenged him.

"It's for the biker crowd, the people that go to the off-road vehicle park. Very rough."

Lizzie sighed. "Okay, maybe I'll try Bertrand's. The food is good, you say?"

"Very good; he is a certified French chef."

"Here in Borrego Springs?"

"Yes, Ma'am."

"Don't call me *ma'am*—I am not that old."

"Yes, Miss."

"I think I'll give Bertrand's a try. He sounds interesting."

"He is quite unusual."

Half an hour later, Lizzie sat at the bar of Bertrand's restaurant. It wasn't exactly what she had expected, but then she wasn't sure what to expect from a French restaurant in Borrego Springs. To put it bluntly, it was more Borrego Springs than French. Located in the back of the town's one and only shopping mall, it had linoleum floors, Formica laminate counters, and imitation wood tables. Lizzie figured scotch was called for to match the surroundings. Bertrand stood behind the bar and recognized her. He smiled, trying to cover up his chipped tooth.

"Mademoiselle, did you enjoy the retreat today?" He put the glass with scotch on ice down in front of her.

"It was . . . different." Lizzie smiled back.

"Different from the regular Borrego Springs offerings. That's why I went."

Lizzie sipped her scotch.

"What do you recommend?" she asked, studying the menu.

"Our special for the holidays is sauerbraten, a tender Southern German roast in vinegar, herbs, and a little sour cream, with spätzle and red cabbage. As an appetizer, I suggest the onion tart."

"Onion tart? That sounds unusual. I'll try that."

Bertrand smiled and disappeared, leaving Lizzie to inspect the other customers. Next to her sat a woman in her mid-forties in extremely tight jeans, causing her belly to bulge over the waistband. She had shoulder-length dyed and permed hair that needed washing and smudged eye makeup. Over her other shoulder, Lizzie detected a middle-aged man in a bleached-out baseball cap sporting the San Diego Padres logo. His plaid shirt with paint stains hung over his baggy jeans. Lizzie quickly directed her attention back to her scotch. The glass doors opened, letting in cold desert night air, as well as Jerome and Hilde Schlesinger. They noticed Lizzie at once and invited her to join them for dinner, which she gladly accepted.

They ordered and made some small talk, "What is a pretty young girl like you doing at a Borrego Springs retreat like ours?" Hilde said jokingly. Seeing Jerome's lightly disapproving frown, she quickly added, "Most of our participants are a bit older and of a slightly different type."

Lizzie decided to put her cards on the table.

"I have to admit, I didn't read your book and I have no special affinity for cosmic events like the winter solstice. I don't think I ever noticed it before. My idea of the longest night was one without any parties. I'm here for the singular reason that Ramon Matus was found with a letter from you in his pocket when he died. He was my boyfriend, and I want to know, what was the connection between you and him?"

"Aha!" Jerome nodded sagely.

"Well, what did you write in that letter?" Lizzie insisted.

At this point the waitress, in jeans and a white T-shirt, brought their dinner. Three plates were heaped high and smelled divine, even though the presentation left a bit to be desired.

"Would you like some ketchup?" the waitress asked Lizzie between chewing her gum.

All three declined, horrified.

"*Guten Appetit,*" Hilde said cheerfully and tucked into her sauerbraten.

Lizzie was annoyed. She was finally getting closer to the purpose of her visit and then they put all this heavy food in front of her nose, interrupting their conversation. After a few bites, however, she softened. The roast melted on her tongue and the slightly sour flavor tingled her taste buds. The Schlesingers smiled.

"We don't come here for the ambience, but the food is amazing," declared Hilde.

After a few moments of silent eating, Jerome began. "What was in that letter? I have thought about it a lot. Did it play any part in what happened to Ramon Matus?" He took a sip of Bordeaux wine. "I was a great admirer of your friend. As you might expect, I'm not an expert in art, and I'm sure you understand his work much better than I. What struck me was Matus's intuitive use of natural materials to represent complex concepts."

Lizzie raised her eyebrows.

"I have studied the Yaqui cosmology and I wanted to talk to Ramon about it," Schlesinger continued. "The Yaqui universe consists of five realms, or worlds, all interacting but also existing parallel and simultaneously with each other. They are the desert/wilderness world; the mystical/non-rational world, also called the *nagual*; the dream world; the night world; and finally, the flower world."

"Ramon did installations about each of these worlds," Lizzie confirmed. "Before he died, he was working on a flower piece. I saw the drawings at his studio. It looked like a funeral to me."

Schlesinger nodded again. "Each of these worlds acts like a portal into the next Yaqui dimension."

"Ramon created these portals so his viewers could experience the Yaqui worlds," it dawned on Lizzie.

"His desert and darkness installation had a big impact on me," admitted Schlesinger. "Personally, I am very interested in the connection between my spiritual and emotional laws and the natural world. Hence the nature walk and my choice to present this retreat during the winter solstice."

Lizzie rolled her eyes.

"I know you weren't keen on the walk," he added with a smile. "But that's because I don't have your boyfriend's magic touch to create immediate, powerful experiences like he did. I'm just a Jewish intellectual. I can explain concepts, but he could create experiences."

Lizzie nodded. "That's what his art is all about: a direct connection between the viewer and the work," she said.

"Exactly. I wrote in the letter that I wanted to talk to him about the Yaqui worlds. I wanted his permission to use some of his images in my next book."

Lizzie felt immediately furious with this Jewish intellectual. He had wanted to exploit Ramon and his artistic heritage for his own profit, she realized. "Why can't you use images from your own culture? Some Jewish symbols!"

Jerome smiled. "I respect your anger. It was not my intention to use Ramon. I wanted to collaborate with him, quote his work in my next book, but I don't think he was interested."

"No, I think not. Ramon was a conceptual artist, not some Yaqui Indian shaman, like you seem to suggest." Lizzie steamed. This guy had nothing to contribute; he just wanted to use Ramon and his Indian roots. He didn't understand a thing about him. Coming to the desert to find Schlesinger had been a dead end.

"Mr. Schlesinger, you indeed know nothing about art and nothing about Ramon. You completely missed the point. Whether Ramon was a Yaqui Indian is quite irrelevant. He was a great artist." Lizzie got up. "I think I'll just go and look at the stars," she declared angrily, threw some money on the table, and stormed out.

Jerome smiled sadly. Hilde got up to follow Lizzie, but Jerome held her back.

"Let her go. She's a smart girl. She'll figure it out."

"Whatever you say, dear. I just don't want her to drive after drinking two glasses of scotch. She's upset and can get into an accident."

Bertrand came over to the table in alarm.

"No, Bertrand, there's nothing wrong with the food. It's delicious as usual," Jerome said, trying to calm him. "Just a little disagreement."

Bertrand nodded. Disagreements he understood. People not liking his food—now, that would've been a disaster.

Lizzie drove into the night, past Christmas Circle with its sad illuminated plastic nativity figures, then straight out of town. She stayed on S1 toward the off-road vehicle park. She was furious. The conversation with Schlesinger had gotten her nowhere. All she had found out was that Schlesinger wanted to exploit Ramon and that Ramon wanted nothing to do with him.

And yet, it was interesting, what he had said about the Yaqui worlds: the desert world, the night world, the mystical realm, the dream and the flower worlds. It explained Ramon's work. She would look at it now from a new perspective, maybe even tell Vega Stern about it.

Lizzie drove past the deserted airstrip on the right, bathed in cold moonlight. The full moon cast a silvery sheen onto the road and the desert scrub beyond. Otherwise, the night was black.

She drove too fast on the straight and empty road. She couldn't take her foot off the gas pedal. It felt good to take out her anger with speed. A curve emerged in the headlights. Lizzie tore the steering wheel around. Her small car skidded across the road, not heavy enough to stay on the tarmac. Lizzie tried to brake. An ugly screeching sound interrupted the quiet night. The car ran right into the desert scrub, kept skidding, and slid down into a ditch, where it finally came to a halt. As if in slow motion, Lizzie was thrown forward against the steering wheel. Her seat belt restrained her, but a sharp pain somewhere in her abdomen pierced her awareness. She brought her arm up to shield herself from the impact. Suddenly all was quiet. Lizzie lifted her head. She groaned, as she unraveled herself from the steering wheel. The door still opened. A good sign. Slowly, she crawled out of the car, holding onto its side for support.

She sunk down onto the desert sand and leaned against the car, to slow her breathing. Touching her arms and torso, she tried to assess any damage. She winced at a bruise on her side, but nothing seemed broken. At least there was no blood. What about the car? She turned around to examine her Miata, which was smoking and hissing in the dark. It didn't sound good. The fender was bent, and who knew what the brakes and the tires looked like? What now? Lizzie pulled her purse out of the open car door and searched for her phone. Good, it still worked. She placed a call to La Casa Del Zorro.

"My name is Lizzie Cantor. I'm a guest and I had a car accident." In response to the concierge's questions, she said, "I'm okay. I'm a bit past the airstrip in a ditch on the right side of the road."

Thanking the person for the hotel's help, she hung up and felt a bit calmer. They were on their way.

Clear and chilly night air streamed into her lungs. She leaned back and squinted up at the sky. There were stars, sparkling, cold and distant. Stars, millions of them. Straight overhead she could even see the fuzzy strip of the Milky Way. The stars back in the city were hazy and faint. This night sky wasn't like anything she had ever seen; it was brilliant. A few constellations, the easy ones, emerged after a few minutes of staring at the tumble of stars: the Big Dipper, and Orion's belt with its three super-bright stars in a row.

Congratulations, Schlesinger, she thought. *I'm looking at the sky on the winter solstice after all.* Leaning on the hood of her convertible, head back, she let the sparkling and twinkling sink in. *But it's not because of you, Jerome. It took a car accident to make me slow down and see.*

Some stars seemed to blink and then disappear, or maybe those were satellites. Some seemed to get brighter or fainter. More emerged as she kept looking. Lizzie felt very small and suddenly very cold. She got back into the car. Enough of the light show.

It occurred to her that even though Ramon hadn't answered Schlesinger's letter, he had still carried it in his pocket. He had not thrown it away; he may have planned to meet with Jerome. He hadn't completely dismissed him. Maybe Lizzie would give Jerome a second chance. She wasn't going anywhere in her crashed car anyway.

SATURDAY, DECEMBER 21, 8:30 P.M.

Jerome and Hilde Schlesinger finished their meal in awkward silence.

"I'm worried about the girl running out into the desert in such a state," Hilde finally said.

In Jerome's mind, images of Jewish, Indian, and Christian symbols swirled around in an untidy whirlpool. Both were glad when the sauerbraten was finally consumed and they could ask for the check. The restaurant had been emptying out and they were just about the last customers.

Besides them, only a dark-haired man, whose white shirt was unbuttoned a little too far down, sat at the bar. He was engrossed in an intense exchange with Bertrand. Jerome snatched only a fragment of their conversation, the words "goddamn artist" exclaimed in a raised voice. Bertrand responded by nodding over in their direction. The man looked around, made an effort to smile, and was silent.

"Let's go take our winter solstice walk," Hilde said, breaking the uncomfortable silence.

Passing the bar on their way out, Jerome caught a whiff of strong, sharp aftershave. As the glass doors closed behind them, they heard raised voices inside.

SATURDAY, DECEMBER 21, 8:40 P.M.

"Are you out of your mind coming here while I have customers?" The usually mild-mannered Bertrand raised his voice angrily.

"I need to know what is going on. I get pressure from above about the mess in Borrego Springs, and I don't even know what happened. The police are all over this thing."

"What do you think? A well-known artist was killed. He wasn't just some no-name Mexican illegal. He had friends in high places," Bertrand replied.

"Yes, that's the problem—too much attention, reinforcements along the border, high-alert status. I mean, how am I going to explain that?"

"I don't know. I can't help you there." Bertrand turned around to the bar shelves behind him.

"Do they have any leads?"

"Not as far as I know. But it would be a good idea to give them something. I made up a story about two men coming here on the night of the murder."

"We didn't murder no goddamn artist."

"Don't tell me what you did or did not do. I don't want to know. My advice is, come up with two men." Bertrand had lowered his voice to a whisper.

"To take the fall?" the man asked.

"That's your problem how you want to play it. But it's the only way to get them off your back."

"That's not going to go over well."

"After what you pulled here tonight, you'd better come up with something. Those people will remember you."

"I'm nervous. You understand?" the man hissed.

"How do you think *I* feel? I can't go anywhere. I'm a sitting duck." Bertrand knew the feeling.

"Alright, I'll figure something out. Just keep your eyes and ears open."

"Always."

The man finished his drink, slammed the glass onto the counter, and walked into the night. Bertrand was finally alone. He poured himself a large glass of whiskey.

39

DECEMBER 21-DECEMBER 22

Greg and the boys returned from their hike as the sun set. Vega had been hysterical with worry, thinking they might have gotten lost in the caves of the badlands.

"There is a killer on the loose!" she shouted. "This is no time to take unnecessary risks."

"Calm down, Vega. Everybody's fine," Greg said, unconcerned. "We can take care of ourselves—right, boys?"

The boys nodded proudly, still flushed from their adventure.

"You guys revel in your dangerous adventure, then. I'm going for a walk to see the stars on winter solstice." Vega walked out into the night.

She looked for the faraway galaxies surrounding the star Vega in the constellation Lyra, while thinking about Schlesinger's Law #10: *There are always more than two solutions to a problem—it is never "either/or," but rather "as well as." If a problem can't be solved, let it go. Give it to the cosmic washing machine.*

She decided to throw all her questions and confusion about Ramon's death into the cosmic washing machine. She imagined it as a giant whirlpool out in space, where her own little worries and concerns were insignificant. They'd get churned over and sorted out while she slept. She also threw in her fears for her sons, wanting them to be safe while navigating growing up in America. Sending off all these worries, she felt calm, and once she got back to their hotel room that night she fell asleep right away.

Vega had a strange dream. She saw Ramon smiling at her, while warm sunlight reflected off his black hair. He seemed to be lying in a hammock and he appeared very much at peace.

～

Waking up, Vega told Greg about her dream.

"I dreamt about Ramon last night. I think he is in a good place, wherever he is."

"Is he in the afterlife?" asked Stevie, who had overheard her and was very interested in ghosts.

"I think so," replied Vega hesitantly.

"What does it look like there?" Stevie wanted to know.

"In my dream, it looked like a sunny resort."

"Oh, that's boring. No fog or hell hounds?" Stevie was visibly disappointed.

"Not in this version," Vega replied, but Stevie and the rest of the family had already lost interest in her dream.

Vega put on her bathing suit and went out to La Casa Del Zorro's swimming pool. The water was warmer than the crisp morning air. Steam rose from the pool as the first rays of the rising sun reached the tips of the palm trees.

She thought about the shadow Ramon's death had cast on the art community, on Borrego Springs, on his family, even on her own family. She thought about his artwork, particularly the rock casting the colorful shadow. As Vega swam her laps, she caught a glimpse of the insight she'd had during yesterday's meditation. There was a connection, a foreshadowing.

I think I can understand where Ramon was coming from, she realized. *It's all a matter of cause and effect. If I look carefully at the effect of Ramon's death, I will be able to trace it back to its origin.* This one event has created a huge ripple effect.

The effect on Schlesinger was good; it had improved his business. The effect on Borrego Springs was also good. It had brought tourists and journalists to the area. La Casa Del Zorro had more guests. Ramon's art had increased in value. The Border Patrol had increased security along the border. Vega was not sure if that was good or bad. She assumed it was bad for the drug cartels, which was good for the rest of the world, but it was bad for the migrants, who would be intercepted even more frequently. At least fewer migrants would die of exposure with more frequent patrols. Ramon's death might improve the fate of the migrants and draw attention to their plight.

Vega remembered her dream and suddenly it became clear to her what had happened to Ramon. She jumped out of the pool and ran inside.

"I think I know what happened," she told her surprised family. "I must go to the police immediately."

40

SUNDAY, DECEMBER 22, 9:00 A.M.

R aoul had *huevos rancheros* for breakfast at the cantina in Cataviña and then began his drive home. He tried to reach Tina on his cell phone after charging it during breakfast, but of course there was no service. He might make it home that night, but he was far down the Baja peninsula. He'd probably have to stay over in Ensenada, maybe at his cousins' house, and then get back the next morning. Raoul drove fast, though not recklessly. He was tired, but at peace. As he traveled back through the cactus gardens, the saguaros seemed to stand in silent salute. At El Rosario he filled up the tank again, got lunch, and then made good time through San Quintín.

By early dusk Raoul reached the outskirts of Ensenada. His cousins Diego and Francisco lived south of the city in the Guadalupe Valley in San Antonio de las Minas. Their parents owned a three-acre plot of land with several buildings. One was a garage, where father and sons fixed cars. There was the two-story main house with the kitchen and the living and dining rooms and two bedrooms upstairs, and then there was Francisco and Diego's shack. They had built it themselves. It was an odd assortment of found doors and window frames all set helter-skelter into wood-framed walls covered in drywall the brothers had never bothered to paint. But it gave them some privacy and a measure of independence from their parents.

Raoul expected to sleep in the shack on the worn sofa, after a few beers and maybe a couple of songs sung by Diego accompanying himself on his guitar. What the shack lacked in style, it made up for with the view from the porch the brothers had cobbled together. The covered porch looked out over the wild Guadalupe Valley toward the west. Raoul and Ramon had enjoyed many beautiful sunsets over the hills there in the past. It would be good to see Diego and Francisco. He hadn't heard from them in over a year.

As Raoul drove up the dirt road to the main house he saw the outline of his father's brother, Antonio, against the brightly lit window. Hearing the car approach, he stepped out of the door to greet the unexpected visitor.

"Raoul! What brings you here? It is good to see you. It has been too long. How is your father? Sandra, set another place at the dinner table —Raoul is here!"

Antonio embraced his nephew. Sandra and Francisco came running out and greeted him happily.

During the dinner of *carne asada* with rice and beans, Raoul told them about his journey. They had heard about Ramon's death and were devastated by it. Francisco seemed particularly distressed. They understood that Raoul had to take some time off to get over the loss. Sandra told them to go to the shack; she would clean up with Antonio.

"Where is Diego?" Raoul asked Francisco, after they had settled in on the porch with a few beers.

"He's on vacation," Francisco said.

"Vacation?" Raoul was surprised. "What does he need a vacation for? And how can he afford one? Where did he go?"

"He went to the Yucatán. He's always wanted to see the Mayan pyramids."

"Why didn't you go together?"

"Someone had to help Dad in the garage."

Raoul sat silently for a few minutes. Something about this story didn't make sense. Diego had never taken a vacation in his life. He adored Ramon to the point of worship and helped whenever possible with his installations. He'd even grown out his hair to resemble his cousin. Diego was not an artist, but he was a good musician.

"Does it have anything to do with Ramon's death?"

"Diego was very upset, as you can imagine."

"But how could he afford a vacation? How long has he been gone?"

"Just a couple of days. He saved up. It was his Christmas wish to see the pyramids."

"Christmas wish? Francisco, what's up? Why don't you tell me what's really going on."

"It's complicated."

"I've got time." Raoul took a sip of beer, determined to wait his cousin out.

"Something went wrong. Diego had to get away for a while."

"What went wrong? Are you still smuggling stuff across the border?"

"I can't talk about it."

"Francisco, it's too dangerous. You don't know who you're dealing with. Look at what happened to Ramon."

"Yes, what did happen to him? Have you really thought about that?"

"What do you think I did these past days?"

"You thought about your loss and you thought about Ramon, how he used to be. But did you really think about what happened to him?"

"What are you trying to say, Francisco?"

"Who murdered him?"

"How am I supposed to know? I don't even know what he was doing out there in the desert."

"Raoul, you just think about yourself and wallow in your grief. You don't look further."

"That is very unfair. What are you hiding from me?" Raoul got up in anger. He wanted to challenge Francisco. What did he know?

"You don't understand anything. You live in your safe and pleasant San Diego. You don't know what it's like here." Francisco sounded bitter.

"Then tell me what's eating you up. What happened to Diego?"

"I wish I could."

"Did he smuggle some illegals across? Drugs?"

"No, he didn't." Francisco looked out over the moonlit valley and took another sip of beer.

"Then how did he get into trouble?"

"I just told you."

"Oh, so he refused. I see. And the cartels didn't like that, is that it?"

"You see nothing."

"I'm your cousin, Francisco. We've known each other all our lives. We lost my brother, your cousin. We need to stick together. What's going on?"

"You're coming here out of the blue, in your shiny truck, demanding answers. I'll give you an answer. You don't really give a damn about us and how we survive down here." Francisco stood over Raoul, pointing his finger at his chest.

Raoul got up and took Francisco by the shoulders, ready to shake him. "Don't threaten me and don't accuse me. We are family. I want to help, and I deserve to know what's going on."

"Let go of me, Raoul." Francisco shook him off. "Don't touch me. Go back across the border, which you can cross so easily. Leave me alone." He turned and stormed off into the night, leaving Raoul behind.

Raoul was seething. He had no idea what had gotten into his cousin. Obviously, Francisco wasn't going to tell him. He sould just drive home and arrive in a couple of hours. The border was easier to cross at night than in the morning. He'd have some time to think about what Francisco had said, and what he hadn't said, before getting there.

41

MONDAY, DECEMBER 23, 9:30 A.M.

At the Borrego Springs Sheriff's Department, Mai Ling had brought in extra chairs for the meeting and put water bottles next to each of them. She had also made folders with copies of all the reports for everybody and put them on the seats. She wanted this meeting to be productive. Sheriff Thompson, as usual, was behind his desk. In front of him sat Chief Detective Vincelli and Officer McInness from Border Patrol. Detective Henderson and Deputy Ling were seated on narrow chairs squeezed in on either side of the desk.

"Good morning, gentlemen," boomed Thompson, conveniently forgetting that Ling was also present. "I hope you had a good weekend and are ready to tackle this investigation. We all want to get home for Christmas." He smiled expansively. "I assume you all read the reports, so where shall we begin?"

Vincelli cleared his throat and began.

"We discovered that Ramon Matus's girlfriend, Lizzie Cantor, may have had an affair with Ramon Matus's brother, Raoul, who was seen by an eyewitness entering Cantor's apartment before dawn the day after Matus's death. Raoul has since gone missing."

"After confronting Liz Cantor here at the Casa Del Zorro, she admitted seeing the brother that night but claims their encounter had no significance and that she doesn't know where Raoul is at the moment," added Henderson. "And neither does his wife, by the way. There is a missing person report out on him, but we assume he has slipped south of the border."

"It doesn't look good for Raoul. He is gone, twenty thousand dollars are gone, and he had a thing with his now dead brother's girlfriend." Thompson voiced his favorite theory. "Looks like he popped his brother, took the money and the girl, and ran."

"But the girl is still here. She's at the Casa Del Zorro right now," said Vincelli.

"That still leaves the money as a motive. Maybe he is planning to rendezvous with the girl later on." Thompson was not wavering.

"After talking to Ronald Cantor, Liz Cantor's father and Ramon's art dealer, I learned that Ramon could have easily saved up twenty thousand dollars from his art sales over a period of time," said Vincelli.

"Twenty thousand dollars isn't a lot. It wouldn't get the killer very far." Deputy Ling said, unconvinced of the money as a motive.

"And why did Ramon withdraw that amount on the night he was killed, unless he planned to buy drugs?" McInness finally contributed to the conversation.

"Maybe he was blackmailed?" Thompson wanted to hold on to his theory.

"About what? Ramon didn't have an adulterous affair. His brother Raoul did." Henderson made a frustrated gesture.

"Does Raoul have an alibi for the time of the murder?" Thompson leaned forward in his chair and nodded in Henderson's direction.

"We weren't able to ask him, since he's missing, but his wife says he was home," Henderson answered.

"Not much of an alibi, in my opinion," said Thompson.

"But it's airtight and unbreakable, due to spousal privilege," Vincelli corrected him.

Thompson grunted. "There is also the matter of the letter by Jerome Schlesinger in Matus's pocket. We interviewed Schlesinger here at the Casa Del Zorro, and his alibi is also pretty flimsy. Claims he didn't know the artist, but the fact that he was in such close proximity is suspicious, to say the least."

"It turns out that not only Jerome Schlesinger, but also Vega Stern, who has written a museum exhibition essay about Ramon Matus, is staying at the Casa Del Zorro this week." Deputy Ling wanted to point out at least one other unusual coincidence.

"One explanation for all these connections would be that Matus was on his way to meet with Schlesinger and maybe Stern, when he was intercepted," said Vincelli.

"Intercepted by whom?" Thompson asked.

"An informant told us that a transfer of drugs or illegals took place that night here in Anza-Borrego. I still have to find out more about who was involved. In the meantime, we have stationed reinforcements along the border," stated McInness.

"What if Ramon Matus planned the whole scene here in the Canyon Sin Nombre as an installation, to draw attention to the plight of the migrants and to his own art?" Deputy Ling speculated.

"And got himself killed in the process?" Thompson asked.

"Maybe he got in the way of coyotes or human traffickers. They felt threatened and killed Ramon," Ling said, to explain her theory.

"A dead artist is better than a live one. When I talked to Ronald Cantor it sounded like demand for Matus's work is going through the roof since he died and he had no qualms about cashing in. He opened a memorial exhibition of his work the day after his body was found," Vincelli said.

"That's bad taste, and if anything it makes Cantor a person of interest, but he has a unshakable alibi. He was in Los Angeles at an art opening with dozens of witnesses, as was his daughter, Liz," reported Ling.

"Should we consider Schlesinger and Vega Stern as suspects?" asked Henderson.

"We can't rule them out. They were both at hand, they have no alibis to speak of, and they were connected to the victim," said Vincelli.

"Perhaps we need to investigate them further. Both were admirers of Ramon Matus's work. But Schlesinger didn't appear to benefit from

Matus's death, and neither did Vega Stern," Ling said, drawing a stern look from Thompson.

"I read Vega Stern's essay," said Henderson with a wince.

"Any good?" joked Thompson.

"It's probably on the level of the *Borrego Sun*," said Henderson. Everybody except Ling laughed.

"Our top priority is to find Raoul Matus," Thompson resumed. "He could fill in the missing pieces. And we need to find Ramon Matus's car. He drove a red Toyota pickup truck."

Both Thompson's and Vincelli's cell phones rang simultaneously. Thompson got up and held his phone to his ear with his giant hand, which seemed to crush the small device. "What?" he shouted. We'll be right there." Looking up at the assembled officers, he announced, "Gentlemen, our main suspect has just arrived back home!"

Vincelli also jumped up, grabbing his phone with one hand and his jacket with the other. He walked toward the window for better reception. Within a minute, he finished his conversation and turned back to the table. "Raoul Matus came home in the early morning hours today. His wife just confirmed. Police are bringing him in to the police station in downtown San Diego as we speak and he will be ready for interrogation as soon as we get there."

"I'm going to San Diego. I can't wait to get my hands on that son of a bitch. McInness, I would still keep the reinforcements in place at the border," Thompson called out as he stormed to the door.

Henderson got up and quickly followed his boss outside.

McInness and Ling watched the meeting disintegrate. This certainly put a new spin on the case. She pushed her way through to Thompson.

"The winter solstice retreat is over today. Can we release the participants so they can go home for the holidays?" she asked urgently, knowing that it would be just like Thompson to forget about the people until after Christmas.

"If we have their addresses and phone numbers you can let them go," he said impatiently. "Now that we have Raoul."

Ling was already on the phone with Hilde Schlesinger, telling her to make the announcement at the end of their session.

Thompson joined Vincelli and Henderson in their car, folding his huge frame into the backseat for the trip to San Diego. As Deputy Ling watched them drive off into the chilly and clear desert morning through the open door, she remembered the sad and confused Raoul she had driven along this road to the morgue to identify his brother. It was hard to imagine him as a cold-blooded murderer.

42

MONDAY, DECEMBER 23, 1:00 P.M.

Tired and confused, Raoul sat at the bare table in the empty interrogation room at San Diego Police Headquarters, waiting. He had a plastic cup of water in front of him, nothing else. When Detective Vincelli and Deputy Sheriff Thompson finally entered, Raoul barely looked up.

"Mr. Matus, we have a few questions. Please be advised that anything you say can be held against you in a court of law," Vincelli began.

"I've got nothing to hide," was Raoul's tired answer.

Vincelli sat down across the table from Raoul and switched on the recording device, entering the time, date, and persons present.

"That's good to hear, Mr. Matus," Thompson said in a mocking tone. "You have evaded the authorities for three days, but you've got nothing to hide?"

"I didn't evade the authorities. I wasn't aware you were looking for me."

"Where were you on December eighteenth between five and nine o'clock in the evening?" Vincelli asked calmly.

"You think I killed my brother?"

"As a matter of fact, I do." Thompson played the role of the bad cop perfectly. "What makes you ask that?"

"I know that's when he died. They told me at the morgue. On Wednesday night I was at home with my family. We had dinner and then I went to bed. I get up early."

"Not much of an alibi, is it?" bellowed Thompson. "Since you get up so early, can you tell us where you were on Friday, December twentieth, about four thirty in the morning?"

"I must have been at home ready to get up and go to work," Raoul answered.

Thompson raised himself up to his imposing height and stood right in front of Raoul, leaning in so their faces were only a few inches apart.

"Let me jolt your memory. You were seen entering Liz Cantor's apartment at that time."

"Oh yes, on Friday. I did visit her. She was very upset about my brother's death. I went to talk to her. I'd done a bad job telling her about Ramon's death over the phone. I owed it to her to at least speak to her in person."

"You did a bad job? How did you make it up to her?" Thompson sneered.

Vincelli sat very casually in his chair, legs crossed, and watched the exchange with an amused expression.

"So how did you do it?" Thompson repeated.

"I tried to comfort her."

"That's not what she tells us. Mr. Matus, let's just get this straight. We're not in preschool here. You screwed your brother's girlfriend the night after he was murdered. That's not exactly what I would call brotherly love. How long had it been going on between the two of you?"

Raoul crumbled on his seat. Vincelli grinned.

"You misunderstand. It was nothing. It never happened before and never will again. That was the first and last time. Please don't say anything about this to my wife. She is upset enough as it is. My son was in the hospital, and my mother's very ill. Tina has enough to worry about."

"You're right. She does, Mr. Matus. We can't promise that she won't find out about this. Maybe you should have thought about your wife as you were comforting your brother's girlfriend," suggested Thompson. "And if your affair with Ms. Cantor was so unimportant, then why did you disappear immediately afterwards?"

"I know it looks bad, but I needed to think."

"I agree with you, it does look bad," confirmed Thompson.

"Where did you go and whom did you meet?" Vincelli asked reasonably.

"I drove down Baja. I didn't meet anybody. I just needed to be alone for a couple of days. Deal with what happened."

"What did happen, Mr. Matus? We know you screwed your brother's girlfriend. Did you kill him first?"

Matus stared at him wide-eyed, clutching his water glass.

"What did you do during those two days you spent in Baja?" Vincelli asked calmly.

"I just drove down to Cataviña, spent some time in the desert, cleared my head."

"That's a good one. You expect us to believe that? After all the lies we already heard? What did you do with the twenty thousand dollars?" Thompson still stood over Raoul, looking down on him.

"What twenty thousand dollars?"

"Don't play the simpleton, Mr. Matus. We know you have the money."

Vincelli raised his eyebrows. Thompson was doing a pretty good bad-cop routine.

"I don't know what money you're talking about," Raoul repeated.

"Don't worry; we will find out. It's easy enough to track your spending. Did you spend it on Liz Cantor?"

"Can you leave Liz out of this, please?"

"No, absolutely not."

"Did you see or talk to anybody while you were in Baja, someone who could account for your whereabouts?" asked Vincelli.

"Well, the receptionist at the Hotel in Cataviña. And my cousin in Ensenada. I visited him on the way back."

"We'll need his name and phone number. Did your cousin have any contact with your brother?"

"Sometimes he worked with Ramon on projects. We have two cousins in Baja, Francisco and Diego. Diego is on vacation in the Yucatán right now. I talked to Francisco."

"Did your brother use drugs?" Vincelli switched gears.

"No, never. He was a mindful man. He didn't want to muddle his mind."

"Was he involved in any drug-dealing business?"

"Of course not. He was an artist."

"Look, Mr. Matus," Vincelli said reasonably. "You know your brother best. What could he have done out in the desert on Wednesday night and why did he have twenty thousand dollars with him?"

"He must have been working on an installation, and he probably planned to pay someone off."

"Paying someone off for what?" Vincelli followed up.

"Materials, for work done. Look, I don't know. I really need to get back to my family."

"Not so fast, my friend. Your family will have to do without you for a little longer," Thompson said, sounding triumphant.

"You can't just keep me here."

"Just watch us," said Thompson with a satisfied grin.

"Why don't you ask Lizzie about Ramon's work and where he went? Did you check his phone records for that night?" Raoul said desperately.

"Now he is telling us how to do our job," said Thompson.

"Ramon received a call from a Mexican number. We weren't able to track it; it belonged to a disposable cell phone," Vincelli explained.

"I loved my brother. I'd do anything to help find who did this. I'm very upset about his death and that's why I left. I wasn't trying to run away," pleaded Raoul, close to a breaking point.

"Yes, so you said. Upset enough to screw his girlfriend."

Raoul broke down, sobbing.

43

MONDAY, DECEMBER 23, 1:00 P.M.

At the conclusion of the retreat, Lizzie hopped into her convertible. It had been patched up in the Borrego Springs auto shop. The fender still looked bent from the accident, but at least it was running. She decided to avoid the freeways, and instead drive east to the Salton Sea and then north past Palm Springs to Los Angeles, where she planned to spend Christmas with her parents. There would be parties at the gallery and dinners with collectors and plenty of diversion, which is what Lizzie craved after all that soul-searching at the retreat.

The afternoon air was crystal clear, warm and sunny. Lizzie enjoyed letting her hair fly in the wind while cruising along the S22 east in a straight line. Soon she saw the Salton Sea shimmering like a mirage in the distance, like heat waves rising from the desert floor. With a lingering glance at the placid surface of the salty waters, she took a left onto the 86 north through Mecca in the Coachella Valley.

The last day of the retreat had been devoted to spiritual law #10: *There are always more than two solutions to a problem—it's never "either/or," but rather "as well as." If a problem can't be solved, let it go. Give it to the cosmic washing machine.*

At first Lizzie found the concept of the cosmic washing machine absolutely ridiculous, but then she warmed to it. She imagined it like a giant cosmic whirlpool. You could throw in your problems at night, then go to sleep, and in the morning they'd be ready, clean, and folded. Sometimes letting go and allowing your unconscious wisdom to take over was not a bad idea. Lizzie was going to try it. She'd take her memories of Ramon, her obsession with what happened to him, and put it in the cosmic washing machine. There was nothing more she could do about it anyway. She'd think about other things, maybe go out with friends in LA, maybe even go on a date.

The wind whipped her hair around her face and she smelled the salty air of the inland lake. A date sounded good right now. There was a young artist who showed at her father's gallery. She would probably see him over the holidays. Just having drinks with a person her own age seemed like such a treat after spending three days with the geriatric crowd at La Casa Del Zorro. Lizzie drove a little faster. Her blue convertible zipped along the empty road, purring like a tame panther.

It was good to be alive. Ramon was dead; time to let him go. Lizzie watched a wispy cloud float above the horizon. A red-tailed hawk glided overhead. All was peaceful until her cell phone rang. She fished it out of her purse.

"Hello," Lizzie answered, barely reducing her speed. "Who? Mr. Matus, yes." Lizzie pulled over to the side of the road. Due to the language barrier and the bad reception, Ramon's father was difficult to understand.

"Ramon's body has been released and cremated." Lizzie wondered why Raoul wasn't telling her this information.

"Is there going to be a funeral? . . . At the beach in Coronado. Yes, he would have liked that." Lizzie wiggled in her seat, trying to get a better reception.

"Yes, of course I will come. The day after Christmas . . . Of course I will help . . . Flowers like his last drawings . . . Yes, that's a good idea. I'll call you back from LA. Okay, thank you, Mr. Matus." Lizzie hung up.

So much for letting go.

44

MONDAY, DECEMBER 23, 1:00 P.M.

T he sun stood high in the sky, or at least as high as it was going to rise in midwinter, and the desert fox still had not found any food. He trotted on the gravel ground of the Canyon Sin Nombre, remembering the place where he had found a feast several days ago. Sure enough, his rivals, the turkey vultures, were circling overhead again. The fox sprinted over the hill into the side canyon on the way to the wind caves and saw the prey, lying on the ground. Two bodies this time. His next meal had been secured.

The fox wasn't the only one on his way into the Canyon Sin Nombre. Deputy Ling drove with Vega in her police jeep out of Split Mountain into the flat northern end of the canyon. She had asked Vega before her departure from La Casa Del Zorro to drive with her to the site to see if they could support her theory. Now they were on their way to the Canyon Sin Nombre for a last look to search for clues confirming Vega's theory that Matus had set up the scene as a message, or a "conceptual artwork."

"I still don't understand how a crime scene could be a conceptual artwork," Ling said.

"Any installation done with a purpose and based on an idea can be a conceptual artwork," Vega explained.

"And what was the purpose?"

"To draw attention to the dangers the illegal migrant workers face, and to draw attention to his own work."

"So the artist's own death became part of the work?"

"I assume he was surprised and killed in the process of setting up the installation, proving his point of how dangerous this area is."

"What else was there besides the body to qualify as an art installation?"

"The name of the location, for example. Giving a name to those migrants who remain nameless. But that's what we are here to find out," Vega said.

They approached the spot where only four days ago Ramon's body had been found. Ling had patrolled this area only yesterday afternoon. But something was different today. She looked up and realized the emptiness around them was not complete. The sky above was populated with turkey vultures circling overhead. Ling immediately stopped the car and grabbed her phone and gun. "Stay in the car," she warned, but of course Vega followed. Ling scrambled up the hill toward the wind caves. She felt her heart beating fast, either from the uphill run or because she knew something was seriously wrong.

When they reached the crest of the hill, Vega had a moment of déjà vu. A cluster of black screeching birds had descended onto something on the canyon floor. Ling fired her gun into the air, and the vultures and a fox reluctantly let go of their meal. Their flight revealed two bodies on the exact same spot where the dead artist had lain. Ling ran down the slope to secure the site. These bodies had not been here the day before. Someone had dumped them here last night or this morning.

Ling had to scramble back up to the ridge before she could called for a full crime scene team. Then she called Deputy Sheriff Thompson. He didn't pick up. Of course, he was interrogating Raoul Matus and had probably turned his cell phone off. She tried Vincelli. No luck either. She dialed Thompson's number again and left a message.

"Deputy Sheriff Thompson, this is Deputy Ling. I am in the Canyon Sin Nombre, with Vega Stern. There are two more bodies at the same site where Ramon Matus was found. Male, late twenties, possibly Mexican. It seems they were dumped fairly recently."

She hung up. It felt good to leave this message. It might put a damper on Thompson's enthusiasm to convict Raoul. Ling felt vindicated. She had never believed in Sheriff Thompson's theory.

45

TUESDAY, DECEMBER 24, 8:00 A.M.

U nder a gray and cloudy morning sky, a patrol car rolled up to the small house in the Barrio. The car's back door opened and released a bedraggled Raoul Matus. He slowly made his way to the front door and let himself in. Tina was up making coffee in the kitchen. She came to the door, wearing a light-blue terry cotton bath robe.

"Raoul, for heaven's sake!" she said.

"Tina, I'm so sorry for what I've put you through."

"I'm sorry too." Tina's tone was not bitter, but resigned.

"At least I'm in the clear. Two more bodies were found in the Canyon Sin Nombre. I'm not a suspect anymore."

"Thank God for that."

"We're going to be okay, Tina."

"It's not going to be that easy, Raoul. With your mother being so sick, and after what happened with Jaime . . . What were you thinking, leaving without a word?"

"I tried to reach you, but there was no connection in Baja and my battery was dead."

"I reported you missing, Raoul. On top of everything else, I was worried something had happened to you, something worse than dead batteries."

He tried to give her a hug, but she turned rigid and moved away.

"Go see your mother," she said stiffly.

"Can I please have a cup of coffee first? I haven't slept in days."

Tina poured them each a big mug of coffee. Marcos entered, combed and dressed in a clean shirt and jeans.

"Son, I'm glad you're back," he said formally and clamped his hand on Raoul's shoulder. Raoul gave his father a hug.

"Dad, thank you for helping Tina, and filling in at the business."

The old man took a cup of coffee out to the porch and sat in an old rattan chair watching the light come up, giving Raoul and Tina some privacy in the kitchen.

"Tina, I know it was incredibly hard on you, but I had to do this. I had to go down to Baja. Now I feel stronger, more myself. I had to come to grips with Ramon's death and with my own feelings. I love you and the boys, but I just needed these two days to myself."

"The boys and I needed you too. Jaime was in the hospital with alcohol poisoning. Your mother is really sick. If you love us so much, why didn't you tell us where you were going? Did you even think of us? How we would feel?"

"I'm sorry. I didn't realize you had to deal with so much."

"While you were coming to grips with your feelings, I had to deal with your sick mother, worry about you, and spend the night in the hospital with Jaime. You really let us down. Did it occur to you that I might have feelings too?"

"I'll talk to Jaime."

"Marcos already did."

Juan came into the kitchen wearing his pajamas.

"Dad! You're back. Just in time for Christmas." Juan ran up to his father and gave him a big hug. Raoul grabbed his son and held him tightly.

"I'm so happy to be back with you, Juan. I missed you so much."

"I missed you too. We still have time to buy a Christmas tree. Today is the last day."

"We'll do that, Juan. We'll still find one, don't worry."

"I won't worry anymore, now that you're back."

"I'm just going to say hi to your grandma, okay?"

"And I'll sit with Grandpa for a while."

Raoul went upstairs into his mother's bedroom. She cried when she saw him and wouldn't let go of his hand. Then he went into the boys' room. His older son lay on his bed with earplugs, listening to music.

"Jaime, take those plugs out of your ears and sit up," Raoul said loudly to make himself heard.

Jaime complied silently, glaring at his father in defiance.

"I hear you were in the hospital," Raoul began.

"I hear you were in jail," Jaime shot back.

"What got into you, drinking yourself unconscious? Are you out of your mind?"

"What got into *you*, Dad, leaving us, with Uncle Ramon dead, mom upset, and Grandma sick?"

Raoul smacked his son on the cheek.

"Don't you talk to me like that," Raoul hissed.

Jaime glowered at him. His cheek showed Raoul's bright red handprint.

"I heard your grandpa gave you a good beating," Raoul continued. Jaime nodded.

"I know you were upset. We were all upset, but instead of running off and drinking yourself into a stupor, you should have helped your mother instead of making her life even harder."

"Maybe *you* should've helped her instead of running off!"

Raoul looked at his son sharply.

"I was very upset about your uncle Ramon's death. I went down to Baja to figure things out. I found some ancient caves full of rock paintings, of stars and suns. I want to take you there, together with your brother and mom."

No response from his son.

"You're fourteen; you are old enough to behave like a man. I need to rely on you when I'm not here."

Jaime sulked on his bed.

"You're grounded from now until the summer, and on the weekends you are going to work roofing jobs with me, so you can pay off your hospital bills. Is that clear?"

Jaime stared at his father with hatred.

"You can hate me if you like," Raoul continued. "Part of growing up is learning how to deal with your feelings. I love you very much, even if you don't believe that right now."

Raoul left the room to take a shower, not sure if he had done such a great job dealing with his grief or with his son.

46

TUESDAY, DECEMBER 24, 12:00 NOON

B ertrand was open for business on Christmas Eve. There were always a few strays who didn't have any family or any other place to go. They assembled at Bertrand's like every year and he fed them, and gave them what they really craved: alcohol. It helped him forget his own loneliness and get him through the holidays, which was a challenge every year.

The winter solstice retreat had been a diversion. Nothing more, nothing less. Betsy, the little blond lady from Point Loma, had offered to cook for him for a change. It had been a nice gesture, but in the end it hadn't worked out. Everybody scrambled to leave on Monday afternoon, and she couldn't wait to meet her husband at the airport. Bertrand was actually relieved about it. He didn't want pity from anybody. Never had. He polished his glasses and hoped for a quiet evening. No breakdowns, no fights. That was pretty much his Christmas wish. Maybe he expected too much. The door opened, and McInness intruded on his thoughts.

"Lieutenant, what brings you here on Christmas Eve? Shouldn't you be with your family?" Bertrand greeted him with annoyance. One day of peace a year, was that really too much to ask?

"Bertrand, sorry to intrude," said McInness. At least he had the decency to apologize even though it didn't sound sincere. "But I wanted to hear your thoughts about the latest discoveries in the Canyon-Without-Name."

"What did they find now?" Bertrand asked. "Some dinosaur bones?"

"Now, Bertrand, don't play silly games with me."

"All right, seriously, what did they find?"

"Do I need to spell it out for you? We found your two men from December eighteenth."

Bertrand considered this for a moment. "That's good. Now you can ask them all the questions you want."

McInness looked at him sternly as if he were a stubborn child. "You're still playing games. You know that's not going to work."

"Why not?"

"Because your customers are quite dead."

Bertrand stopped polishing. "Sorry about that. The Canyon Sin Nombre seems to turn into a regular corpse-dumping ground."

"What do you make of it, Bertrand? Two more corpses?"

"I suppose they're a gift for you, Lieutenant."

"How thoughtful. Now who would give me such a lovely Christmas gift?"

"Lieutenant, I'm sure you can figure that out. Did they have anything on them?"

"No, but they looked exactly like the men you described."

"You see? I didn't lie to you."

"All they needed was a red ribbon and a sign, 'We killed Ramon Matus.'"

"I assume that would have been overkill."

"Nice pun, Bertrand."

"Sorry, I didn't mean it like that. Would you like a drink?"

McInness leaned on the bar heavily and placed his hat next to him. "No, I don't want a drink. I'm not in the mood to celebrate."

"Well, Lieutenant, are you going to accept your gift graciously?"

"I'm sorry to admit it, but graciousness has never been my strength, Bertrand."

"You got your murderers. What more do you want?"

"I want the killers who killed the murderers, Bertrand."

"You can never get enough, can you?"

"Not when I'm so close to an answer."

"Lieutenant, your answer is lying right at the bottom of the Canyon Sin Nombre, it seems."

"Bertrand, you aren't being very helpful today."

"You aren't being very grateful today, Lieutenant. It appears you already got all the help you needed. Someone finished your job for you."

"And created another mess."

"Can't you just take what you got and leave it at that? Maybe they got into a fight over the money and killed each other."

"That's brilliant, Bertrand. We should make you a sheriff's deputy. Incidentally, the victims were killed by the same caliber bullets that killed Ramon, probably a Beretta .380 ACP pistol."

"There you go. That's your solution."

"I wish it were as easy as that. There was no gun at the site."

"Don't look a gift horse in the mouth."

47

WEDNESDAY, DECEMBER 25, 1:00 P.M.

The phone vibrated, indicating that a text message had come in.

The man ignored the cell phone in his pocket. He dozed in a hammock on the beach of Akumal, listening to the soothing sound of the waves washing up on the shore and feeling the gentle breeze flowing across his face. His day so far had been relaxing and refreshing, like every day this past week.

He usually started his day with a walk to the small coffee shop on the beach that was little more than an open gazebo. The coffee was fresh, the pastries a day old, and the clientele eclectic: beach bums, diving fanatics, snowbirds from Canada, retired American couples, families on Christmas vacation.

He was the odd Mexican who did not work in the tourist industry or as a fisherman. When he first arrived he was regarded suspiciously, as if any Mexican not serving meals at a restaurant or guiding dive trips had to be a drug dealer or worse. But once he told the locals he was an artist, they started to respect him, and treated him with slightly mystified indulgence. Whatever he did, they assumed, that's what artists do.

In the mornings he snorkeled in the Yal-ku Lagoon, a protected underwater park. He mingled with yellow-and-black-striped sergeant majors, fluorescent blue angelfish, rainbow parrotfish, and inflatable porcupine fish in the slow-motion silent underwater world pierced by sun's rays. He felt at ease in the warm waters of the Mayan reef, its swaying waves much gentler underwater than at the surface. In Akumal Bay he came face to face with loggerhead turtles and stingrays. When he touched the flaky shell of a huge leatherback turtle and looked into the wise eyes of a giant hawksbill turtle, he became aware that the ancient creatures merely tolerated him in their territory. The turtles came here to lay their eggs. That's how Akumal got its name, meaning "Turtle Bay." Divers from all over the world came to these turquoise waters protected by the reef. A shipwreck lay on the bottom of Half Moon Bay. Its coral-encrusted ribs and planks were host to bull and nurse sharks, stingrays, the occasional moray eel, and small silvery barracudas swarming between clusters of pink brain coral.

In the afternoons, he lay in the hammock on the porch of the house he rented at the northern end of Akumal beach next to the Yal-ku Lagoon. He had taken a few excursions to the Mayan pyramids at Chichén Itzá, Tulum, and Coba. He would have been content to just swing in the hammock, listen to the waves. But thoughts about his family, especially his mother, regularly entered his mind and disturbed his peace. He knew she was worried about him, and he wished he could have sent her a message to let her know he was fine. To ease her anxiety. Unfortunately, he couldn't do that. It would have spoiled everything he was trying to achieve, not just for himself but also for the cause of justice. Some issues were simply bigger than family or himself. Some sacrifices had to be made, not just by him but also by his mother. He was confident it would turn out well in the end, but in the meantime a little pain was unavoidable. He sighed.

He was a thinking artist, he explained to one of the divers at the Yal-ku Café over a beer. The diver and his friends accepted that without questions and never asked to see any of his work again. He carried a sketchbook for ideas and diagrams, and that was all he needed.

The phone kept vibrating. With a small grunt, he fumbled for it in the folds of the hammock and retrieved the text message. It was from Francisco.

"Raoul out of jail. Cleared 4 the murder. 2 more bodies found in Canyon Sin Nombre. Jaime in emergency room with overdose. Josefina very sick. Body released and cremated. Funeral and pouring of ashes into ocean planned 4 day after Xmas @ Coronado Beach. Raoul was here looking 4 Diego. R u coming?"

He whistled. While he had been lounging in his hammock living a life of leisure, only occasionally interrupted by climbing a Mayan pyramid or diving into a clear-water cenote, all hell had broken loose back home. He sat up and looked around at the green-blue water, the empty, wide horizon, the few shallow gray rock formations between him and the shoreline. He tried to etch the impression into his mind: the colors, the smell of the salty spray crashing onto the rocks, the sound of the swell.

He didn't have a camera, nor did he need or want one. In his mind he would remember the blues of the sky, the puffy white of a single cloud, the undulating waves, sharp shadows of rocks, silent iguanas standing still like statues on the stony surface. He would have liked to stay longer, but it was time to go home.

48

THURSDAY, DECEMBER 26, 3:00 P.M.

A motley crew of over two hundred people, comprised of artists, family members, neighbors from the barrio, press, and the merely curious, had gathered on Coronado Beach by the lifeguard tower. They did not look as though they had come for a funeral. The art-scene crowd wore black as usual, but they had made an effort to brighten up their attire with colorful scarves and hats, or sneakers, in reference to Ramon's work. Musician friends of the band *Slightly Subversive* had set up a drum kit and two guitarists played barefoot in the sand, accompanied by a pretty girl in miniskirt and boots, who sang into the mike.

The Matus family had supplied food on folding tables: tamales, mountains of tortilla chips and salsa, guacamole, corn tortillas, and *carne asada*. The weather was mild and sky wiped clear of any clouds. Many had taken off their shoes and sat in the sand enjoying the last warm hours of the day. People who had not seen each other in years reunited and new connections were made. Vega Stern and her family were there. Stevie and Daniel built a sand castle and Greg had his arm around Vega's shoulder as they listened to the music.

In the festive atmosphere Vega couldn't avoid the eerie feeling that it was all going according to Ramon's plan. He had set it up this way, even providing the drawings for his funeral flowers. Piles of marigolds and white carnations had been arranged by the water's edge, looking like speckled pyramids. Vega looked over at Lizzie, who stood with an entire contingent from the Cantor Gallery, including her father, Ronald Cantor. Lizzie and her father had supplied the drinks and the flowers. What might Lizzie be feeling? She seemed to be relaxed and composed. Maybe she had let go, or she was "in the moment," as Schlesinger had told them to be. Speaking of which, Schlesinger himself was standing right by the water's edge with his wife, Hilde. Vega walked over to say hello.

"Mr. Schlesinger, even though Ramon's death overshadowed your winter solstice retreat, I still enjoyed it," Vega began.

"Please call me Jerome," Schlesinger interrupted.

"Jerome, some of your laws are quite effective, and they pop into my head as I go about my day. My favorite is the cosmic washing machine. Some problems just can't be solved, at least not right away. Giving them to the cosmic washing machine overnight is a great relief, and it often works. I had an insight that Ramon Matus intended the events surrounding his death to happen," Vega said.

"He provided the drawings for the flowers, didn't he?"

"Yes, and he got all of us together here."

"I believe in the laws, even though I myself can't always follow them perfectly. Today, at this funeral, I find myself comparing my methods with Ramon's images. His are much more powerful than mine. You see, I contradict my own Law Seven: *Don't compare yourself with others. Be happy with who you are.*"

"It's not always so easy," admitted Vega.

"I want to say something to the people here. They all look so young and so full of promise," Schlesinger continued.

"No, dear, you aren't going to speak," interjected Hilde. "You didn't even know the man. Let it go."

Schlesinger smiled. "I'd better listen to my business advisor, or else I get my salary cut."

"Look, Detective Vincelli and Deputy Ling are here," said Hilde to change the subject.

The relaxed party chatter was interrupted as Marcos Matus stepped up to the microphone. He looked drained and haggard, but he stood straight and composed.

"Dear friends and amigos of Ramon, thank you for coming to say good-bye to our son. His ashes will go into the ocean with this boat here. The currents will carry them into the sea, just like his art has spread far and wide. I hope his ideas will continue to spread and he will not be forgotten."

As Marcos paused, the crowd cheered and called out: "Never forgotten!"

"Instead of flower gifts, we are collecting money for the Border Angels, who set up containers with water, food, and clothes in the desert for the migrants. Vega Stern will now say a few words about Ramon's art," Marcos concluded, and stepped aside. Vega took the microphone.

"Ramon Matus was not a man of many words. He didn't need words to express his ideas. He created powerful images and experiences to help us form our own ideas. His art expressed much more than words can say. We have tried to create his final installation here today. The piles of flowers were arranged according to the last drawings he made. We invite you each to come forward and throw one flower into the ocean, with one word that describes what Ramon Matus meant to you. We will send off the flowers with your words on the journey his spirit is about to take."

Vega stepped aside. Marcos and Raoul waded into the shallow surf with the urn. Their pant legs were rolled up. Jaime walked with them, while Josefina watched from a beach chair. She was still weak. Tina and Juan stood right beside her. Marcos threw an orange marigold after them.

"Firstborn son," he said.

"Brother, guide, protector," Raoul added.

Jaime threw a white camellia: "Favorite uncle."

Josefina, with Tina's and Juan's help, threw red and white carnations. "*Mi amor!*" she cried.

"Admiration," was Tina's word, and Juan added, "Hero."

People came forward and hurled words and flowers into the ocean.

"Love!" shouted Lizzie.

"Potential," said Ronald.

Jerome Schlesinger threw a white carnation into the water with the word "Incomparable."

"Inspiration," "Mindbender," "Shaman," "Power," "Shaker," "Creative force," "Supporter of La Raza," "Friend," "Thinker," and "Avant-garde" were some of the other attributions.

Finally, a man in a hat and sunglasses stepped into the water. He threw a red rose. As he took off his hat, long black hair spilled out. He turned to the crowd.

"Alive," he said.

He was the man who came to his own funeral.

Screams of surprise, confusion, and even fear erupted from the gathered crowd. People dropped their flowers and their drinks, and turned to each other in the chaos. Vincelli and Ling stepped forward and into the water. They were glad Vega Stern had alerted them that something unexpected might happen at the funeral.

"Ramon Matus, you are under arrest," declared Detective Vincelli, who pulled Ramon's hands behind his back and handcuffed them.

"What for?" asked Ramon.

"For impersonating a dead person," Vincelli answered promptly.

"Is that a crime?"

"It should be. Let's go—you got a lot of explaining to do."

They turned around and marched Ramon off through the eerily quiet crowd that parted to let them through. Marcos stepped in their way. When he faced his son, flanked by the two law enforcement officers, he slapped him in the face. "How could you?" he spat out, then he turned on his heel and walked away. The people who had just hailed Ramon as "shaman" and "mindbender" now looked at him with suspicion and distaste.

"Ramon, *mi amor*!" cried Josefina.

Ramon tried and to break through the throng of people to reach her, but the officers at his side held his arms with an iron grip. "Mama, don't worry, it will be okay. I will be back soon!" he shouted.

Josefina broke down and fell to the sand, while Marcos hurried to her side.

His eyes fell on Lizzie, who stood thunderstruck on the shore. She wore a long white dress, which was now soaked up to her knees. She covered her mouth with her hand and stared at him. Ramon tried to smile at her. Raoul stood close by and shook his head.

"I'll explain," Ramon said loudly, still calm and composed. "I promise all of you, you will understand."

Vega watched Ramon's straight back as he was led through the throng of people. She had recognized half of his plan, but he had surprised her after all. His elaborate installation even included a resurrection.

The flashlights of the media's cameras went off in rapid succession. They captured a beautiful sunset at a Southern California beach, populated with colorful people amidst piles of flowers. A man who had apparently just returned from the dead was led off in handcuffs. That would make the headlines. What had begun as a routine assignment about the final good-bye of a murder victim, destined for page five or six of their newspaper, had turned into a sensation.

49

THURSDAY, DECEMBER 26, 7:00 P.M.

R amon Matus sat in the same interrogation room at the San Diego Police Headquarters on Broadway where his brother had sat only three days before. Raoul had been drawn, tired, stressed, and rumpled from three days on the road. In contrast, Ramon looked rested and relaxed, dressed in a stylish retro shirt and jeans.

Detectives Henderson and Vincelli were furious about his deception and decided to let him stew a few hours in confinement, or at least until Deputy Sheriff Thompson and Border Agent McInness got there. But Ramon seemed completely unperturbed. He sat calm and composed on the hard wooden chair, as if it were part of a performance. Finally Vincelli, watching from the observation room, couldn't stand it anymore. He decided to go ahead without Thompson and McInness.

"Henderson, we're going in. Let's shake up the smug bastard."

Seated across from Ramon and feeling tenser than he appeared, Vincelli turned on the tape recorder and began:

"Mr. Matus, please state your name for the record."

When Ramon had done so, Vincelli clarified. "Ramon Matus, who was presumably shot dead on December eighteenth in the Anza-

Borrego Desert. Mr. Matus, if not yours, then whose body was found in the Canyon Sin Nombre on December nineteenth?"

"It was my cousin Diego Matus," Ramon answered.

"How did Diego Matus's body get there?" Vincelli was trying hard to stay calm.

"On the evening of Wednesday, December eighteenth, my cousins Diego and Francisco, who live close to Ensenada, brought several illegal immigrants across the border. I did not know about this transaction, but they sometimes work as *polleros* . . ."

"*Polleros?*" Henderson interjected.

"Coyotes, smugglers of illegal immigrants. They guide the workers to a meeting place. From there, they get picked up and transported to fields and factories to work. I don't condone it, but that's what Diego and Francisco do as a sideline. I'm not judging them. At least they get the migrants across alive."

"Mr. Matus, you don't have to give us a speech about the predicament of illegal immigrants," interrupted Vincelli impatiently. "Let's just stay with the facts, please. So, your cousins are human traffickers. What happened next on December eighteenth?"

"My cousin Francisco called me on my cell phone around five thirty in the afternoon. He was very upset. He said, 'Diego is dead. I don't know what to do.' I asked him where he was and told him to wait for me there."

"So you drove out to the desert?"

"Yes."

"Where was the meeting place?"

"I met him in the southern part of the Canyon Sin Nombre, right past the Carrizo Badlands Overlook. A dirt road leads into the canyon, and that's where they were."

"Where did they cross the border?"

"I think somewhere around Jacumba, then they walk towards Ocotillo Wells through the Canyon Sin Nombre."

"They crossed Interstate 8 in bright daylight?"

"Don't ask me the details, I'm not a *pollero*. There are a few places where they can go underneath the freeway. I just know their meeting place was in the Canyon Sin Nombre, and that's where I met Francisco."

"Okay, when did you arrive at the Canyon Sin Nombre?"

"I got there around eight thirty."

"What did you find?"

"I found Diego lying on the ground. He had been shot in the head execution style. His face was a mess. It was terrible." For a moment, Ramon lost his composure and covered his face in his hands.

"Who shot him?"

"Diego and Francisco's contacts shot him, when they delivered the workers."

"Who were those contacts?"

"Two men Francisco had never seen before. He didn't know their names. Different people meet them each time."

"Who sent them?"

"I don't know. I don't think Francisco knows. They were cartel members. You can ask him."

"Why did they shoot Diego?"

"Francisco told me that this time, they wanted him not only to bring the Mexican workers across the border, but also fifty kilos of cocaine. Diego said no. When they arrived without the drugs, the men shot Diego as a warning to Francisco, who is now terrified."

"They shot Diego in front of the workers, and then left with them?"

"Yes, that's what Francisco said. I guess it was a warning for the illegals as well."

"What did you do when you got there?"

"I said to Francisco, 'We can't just let this go. Nothing will happen if we just leave him here.' Obviously, Francisco could not take a dead body back over the border."

"So you dressed Diego as yourself?"

"Yes. Diego and I are close in stature. He admired me, and had let his hair grow out like mine. He was a talented musician, and we were always close." Ramon took a deep breath and paused, obviously overcome by emotions.

"We put my clothes and watch on Diego. I had brought some extra clothes with me. Francisco told me there was a lot of blood." He paused again. "Didn't the watch confuse you?" Ramon asked Vincelli. "The victim's wallet was gone, but his watch was still there."

Vincelli frowned. Originally this detail had puzzled him, and he had brought it up at the first police meeting. But Thompson had brushed it aside, and after that he hadn't really thought much about the watch.

"Your brother used the watch to identify the body. We gave it to him."

"Good, that was the idea."

"What about the letter? Why did you put that into the jacket's pocket?"

"I left the letter in the pocket. Remember, I did not have much time to prepare, and it was already there. I figured it would help identify Diego as myself, since it had my address. I also left my driver's license in the back pocket of my pants, and took Diego's phone and ID."

"Why did you move the body?"

"I wanted the body to be in the Canyon Sin Nombre as a statement. We were trying to give another nameless, dead Mexican a name. The wind caves aren't on the smuggling route, so the police couldn't ignore Diego as just another dead illegal migrant. I also wanted a little more time for me and Francisco to get away."

"What about the money?"

"As soon as Francisco called me, I went to the bank and withdrew twenty thousand dollars. I gave ten thousand to Francisco and used the rest to disappear for a while."

"Where did you go?"

"I drove to the airport in TJ and flew to Cancún under Diego's name."

"What about Francisco?"

"I dropped him off in TJ. He didn't want to go away. He felt he'd endanger his family. He used the money to buy off some cartel members. But he is in danger."

"We'll have to talk to your cousin Francisco, of course. He is the eyewitness to a murder. If he cooperates with us, we'll put him in protective custody. Why didn't you come to the police with this story?"

"What would you have done about another dead Mexican found in the desert? Another statistic, collateral damage in the drug wars?"

"So you wanted publicity?"

"Let's say I wanted to draw some attention to Diego's death and to the situation of people caught in this border conflict."

"And some attention to you and your art," interjected Henderson. He hadn't read that catalogue essay for nothing.

"That was a side effect," Ramon admitted.

"I hope you realize what you did is criminal," exploded Vincelli.

"Which laws did I break?"

"Misleading the authorities and covering up a crime, for starters."

"I didn't cover it up, I made it more visible," Ramon objected.

"There will be a trial," said Vincelli, furious with Ramon's smooth answers.

"I would hope so."

This was obviously part of Ramon's plan. "Another platform for your agenda," Henderson said, exasperated.

"Let's just say another opportunity to draw attention to a problem."

"Mr. Matus," Henderson asked politely, "are you an artist or an activist?"

"Call me an artist-slash-activist. The consequences and interactions resulting from Diego's death, including a trial and a possible backlash against me and my art, are all part of the conceptual-slash-social sculpture, as Joseph Beuys would have called it."

"Social bloody sculpture my ass!" exploded Vincelli. "You're creating a circus."

Ramon Matus smiled pleasantly, and Vincelli realized that he had just become a willing participant-slash-actor in Matus's performance-slash-conceptual-social-sculpture.

50

FRIDAY, DECEMBER 27, 4:00 P.M.

Ramon sat on the stylish mid-century Eames chair in Lizzie's apartment. Mrs. Shmelkes had eyed him suspiciously when he arrived and immediately called Detective Henderson to report that the dead man was back. She was greatly disappointed when Henderson confirmed that they had just released him.

The glass coffee table in front of Lizzie's leather sofa was covered with newspapers. The headlines blared in large letters: "Dead Artist Reemerges at His Own Funeral," "The Artist Who Came Back from the Dead," "Dead Artist Is Alive," and finally "Dead Artist Fools Police, Family, Friends."

"Look at this!" Lizzie screamed. "How could you do this to us, you horrible, despicable, mean monster?"

"Sorry, Lizzie, but it was all part of a conceptual artwork."

"Bullshit!" Lizzie raged. "Playing with people's feelings like this has nothing to do with art. That's just plain cruelty. You almost killed your mother."

"I miscalculated; I didn't think she would take it so hard. But she's fine now."

"I'm surprised the police even let you go."

"They let me out on bail."

"Couldn't you at least have left me a clue?"

"I couldn't. And I wanted to give you a chance to figure out what you really want from me. Are you in love with me, or just with the idea of the Yaqui-Indian-conceptual-artist?"

"You are such an idiot. I was really upset. I made a big effort to find out what happened to you. I even went to that Schlesinger retreat in the desert."

"Thank you, I appreciate your effort. How was it?"

"It was weird. We sat around meditating, listening to Schlesinger's spiritual laws. I just went there looking for clues about you. I couldn't concentrate on that stuff. I can't believe you let us go through with your own funeral!"

"That was pretty amazing. How many people get to go to their own funeral? And how many fantasize about it? Haven't you ever imagined your funeral?"

"No, I haven't imagined my funeral. You're callous. You played with us." Lizzie's voice rose in pitch.

"Lizzie, I had some very specific consequences in mind when I staged my own death. It didn't all quite work out as I thought. There were too many variables."

"What were your intended consequences?" Lizzie asked sarcastically.

"First of all, I wanted to draw attention to Diego's death. I didn't want him to die unnoticed and in vain, just another dead Mexican, a number in a sad statistic. I couldn't prevent his death, but I wanted it to count for something. I knew my death would turn up the heat along the border. There would be questions, and media attention on the desert drama that goes on almost every night."

"Well, congratulations. Two more people turned up dead."

"Probably they weren't even directly responsible for Diego's death. They may have been connected, but the men in charge will most likely never be found."

"Exactly. Why did you put the letter from Jerome Schlesinger in your pocket?"

"It was already there. I hoped it would help to identify the body as me. I also wanted people to think. If they were trying to make a connection between me and Schlesinger, I figured they wouldn't just chalk it up to the untouchable cartels."

"Ramon, Schlesinger became a suspect, and so did your own brother, Raoul!"

"I'm sorry about that. That's something I never imagined would happen. But I'm sure Schlesinger was never in danger of being arrested. Maybe it forced him to think more about his motives in contacting me."

"I talked to Schlesinger. I was furious, because he wanted to use your art for his next book. I told him to use his own culture, and his own symbols."

"Thank you, Lizzie. I actually think he's a good man," said Ramon.

"His spiritual laws are not half bad, when you start thinking about them," conceded Lizzie.

"I didn't anticipate Raoul becoming a suspect. What prompted that?" Ramon asked.

Lizzie blushed slightly. Ramon didn't seem to notice and continued. "I hoped that Raoul would be able to step out of my shadow, become his own man. As his older brother, I've been an obstacle in his life, someone he compares himself to. He felt he couldn't live up to me, even though he did all the right things—the difficult things, like taking over the family business and living with our parents. I owe him. I hope he found out more about himself."

"One of Schlesinger's laws says: *Don't compare yourself to others. Be happy with who you are*," Lizzie remembered.

"There you go. I agree with that."

"What other results did you intend?" Lizzie asked quickly to divert his attention from the subject of Raoul.

"I wanted a wider range of people to look at my art. I knew being dead would cast a long shadow and draw attention to my work."

"My father had a sale the day after your body was found, and apparently he did great. Now he has to share the profits with you, which serves him right."

"I heard. You can't blame him, even though he could have waited at least a couple more days."

"I told him so. Let me get this straight: you staged your own death so that your work would become notorious and more valuable? You played dead for profit and fame?" Lizzie wiggled around on the sofa restlessly and sipped nervously on her glass of wine.

"It was a side effect. Mainly I wanted people to take a second look at my work. What I do, the installations, the constructs and happenings, they don't reveal themselves at first glance. They require a bit of time, a bit of patience, and the willingness to look again."

This sounded almost like Schlesinger's Law # 5: *Slow down the mind enough to hear your thoughts.* Lizzie pointed to the papers strewn on the table.

"People will certainly look again after your resurrection! Maybe not quite so favorably. Read the headlines!"

Ramon laughed. "Controversy is good. I don't need to be loved. I don't want people to look at me as a martyr and a saint. I want them to be critical. Already, there have been two opposing perspectives within the last week. One overly positive one, because of my assumed death, and one negative one, because of my 'resurrection,' as you call it. That's what makes it a conceptual work of art."

"Your resurrection?"

"No, the fact that people look at my artwork totally subjectively. One day they love it, the next they hate it. It sheds light on their thinking process, and that's what I want."

"You manipulated us all."

"I didn't manipulate you, I gave you freedom. Everybody was free to react in their own way. People have choices. Not everybody reacted as I anticipated. Humans are unpredictable. I didn't anticipate that my mother would get so sick."

"And what did you predict for me?" Lizzie asked.

"It was open to discovery. Did you figure out what you want and what you feel?"

"I know that I missed you terribly and that I just couldn't let go."

Ramon looked at her, leaned in, and took her hands in his.

"Where were you this whole time?" Lizzie asked in a gentler voice, after a pause.

"At a beautiful beach in the Yucatán in Mexico called Akumal, because the giant turtles nest in its bay."

"Sounds nice," Lizzie said sarcastically.

"I'm thinking about doing an underwater installation there, once this is all over. Would you like to come with me?" Ramon asked.

"Okay," said Lizzie surprisingly quickly.

Just as Ramon and Lizzie were beginning to enjoy their reunion on the sofa, Ramon's telephone started to vibrate. He glanced at it. "It's Raoul. He can wait," he whispered.

But the phone kept on beeping persistently.

"Go ahead and get it," said Lizzie.

"What's up, Raoul?" Ramon was slightly annoyed about the interruption.

Lizzie watched him answer the call. What was it about this man? Why couldn't she just let him go? He never did what she expected; he never catered to her every need. She was never sure what he thought, and whether he thought about her at all. Maybe that was exactly the attraction. This crazy scheme he had cooked up. It was cruel, and manipulative, and hurtful, but who else besides Ramon could have come up with something like that?

"What? All right, I'll be right there," Ramon said, alarmed.

"What's wrong?" asked Lizzie.

"Francisco has disappeared. I have to go. When I stepped forward, I implicated Francisco. The police wanted to talk to him right away. They may be too late."

"Another consequence of your conceptual art piece?"

"Please, Lizzie, don't be sarcastic. I have to find him."

"You have to find him? You're not a detective. Where are you going to look?" she said, in exasperation that he was just going to leave again. Why was everything else more important than her?

"I have to talk to my aunt and uncle—that's the least I can do."

"If you leave now, don't bother coming back." Lizzie had reached the end of her rope.

Ramon looked at her with surprise. "I'm sorry you feel that way, but I understand. I can't stay. Some things are more important than you and me."

Lizzie threw her wineglass after him.

51

FRIDAY, DECEMBER 27, 8:00 P.M.

Three hours later, Ramon sat with his uncle Antonio and aunt Sandra at the dining room table of the house in Guadalupe Valley like so many times before. This time no food or drink was heaped in front of him. The tablecloth was stained and no vase with flowers had been placed in the middle, as had been his aunt's habit and a point of pride for as long as Ramon could remember. Francisco and Diego's parents sat across from him with gray and haggard faces. Both looked as if they hadn't slept or changed their clothes in days. His aunt's hair hung limply to her shoulders, instead of being held in the neat bun she usually wore. They stared at Ramon blankly, as if they didn't really see him at all. While Josefina had both her sons back, Sandra had lost both of hers. Ramon did not want to stir their grief more deeply, but he had to ask:

"Tell me what happened."

They didn't know. On Thursday, December 26, when they went to the shack to fetch Francisco for lunch, he was gone.

"Ramon, they took him. You have to see the mess. They were looking for something in the shack, and they took him. He was a witness to Diego's murder, so they took him, before he could give out any information," Antonio said in a tired voice.

Ramon thought about his statement at the San Diego Police Station. Detective Vincelli had said, "We'll have to talk to your cousin Francisco, of course." Had he, unwittingly, sealed Francisco's fate? Who knew about his statement? And how had they found out?

As if reading his thoughts, Antonio continued, "Francisco wanted to request police protection after he heard you came back. The FBI contacted him after your statement. They knew he was involved with the cartels, and he was in danger. By then it was too late. The Federales didn't get here fast enough . . ." His voice trailed off.

"I need to go to the shack and look around. See if there are any clues as to where they took him. So the local police haven't been here yet?"

"Two officers from Ensenada. They took one look around and shrugged their shoulders. 'It was the cartel,' they said. 'There is not much we can do.' That was it. Then they left."

"What about Diego?" Sandra suddenly asked. "Who is going to mourn for him, now that he's just another dead Mexican in the desert? Who will care?"

"I will," said Ramon, but he knew it wasn't adequate.

"First Diego, now Francisco. Both of my sons are gone . . ."

Ramon couldn't face her grief. He got up to go to the shack. When he tried to give his aunt a hug, she just sat stiffly on her chair, kneading a handkerchief and looking right through him.

The shack looked like a disaster zone. The sofa was overturned, pillows had been slit open, and feathers had blown about. Books, records, and papers were scattered all over. Ramon righted one of the worn easy chairs and sat down to concentrate.

"Think!" he told himself. "You are a conceptual artist, after all. Of all people, I should be able to think, and see patterns."

He started to look around more slowly and methodically. He had to slow down in order to really see, not just glance around randomly. Diego's guitar had somehow survived the mayhem. It hung untouched and unharmed on its nail on the wall. With an artist's eye, he looked carefully at the few pictures and posters the brothers had assembled. There was the poster of a Carlos Santana concert in Tijuana they had all attended together. A print by Diego Rivera of a peasant woman holding a huge bouquet of white calla lilies had fallen off its nail and lay sideways on the ground. One of his own drawings, a desert landscape he had given his cousins years ago, still hung crookedly on its nail.

Ramon kept scanning the room he knew so well. Something was missing. There was a pattern in this chaos, he was sure of it, but he could not quite put his finger on what it was. He got up and walked around the small living room. What had the intruders been looking for when they came to get Francisco? Drugs, money? Why had they torn the place apart? Why not just shoot Francisco and be done with it? Was his cousin still alive?

Ramon found himself staring at an empty spot on the wall. A picture had once hung there. The empty nail still stuck in the drywall and a slightly lighter rectangle on the wall echoed the shape of the missing picture. Ramon wracked his memory. A photo, a portrait of someone had hung there. Vaguely he could remember the image of a girl. He thought back to the last time he had been here, and recalled what he had seen from the sofa in this spot on the wall.

Slowly it came to him. In his mind the features sharpened and he recognized her. A black-and-white photograph of Francisco's one-time fiancée, Rosa, had once hung in this place of honor.

Rosa had been Francisco's first and great love. They went to school together in Ensenada. When she was sixteen and Francisco was eighteen, he had taken her out in his first car, a blue Chevy Nova, which he had repaired and pieced together from spare parts in his father's workshop.

Francisco patiently courted Rosa, who was shy and pretty, but he did not have enough money to marry her. Eventually, she went north, across the border, to try her luck as a house cleaner. Except she never made it that far. She drowned in the Tijuana River, during an unexpected flood, as she was attempting to wade across.

After her death, Francisco started smuggling illegal immigrants across the border. At least they would arrive alive. And Rosa's picture had hung right across from the sofa, facing north.

What interest would the cartel have in a photo of Rosa? They'd left all the other pictures in place. Ramon examined the nail and the location where the portrait had hung more closely. On the ground underneath, in a pile of blankets and sheets, he found a silver frame. It was the same frame that had held Rosa's image. Someone had carefully removed the photograph and left the empty frame behind. Someone who'd had enough time to loosen the small screws that held the picture in the frame. Someone to whom the photograph of Rosa meant so much, he could not leave it behind.

Ramon sat back in the easy chair and took a deep breath. He knew what his discovery meant, but he didn't want to believe it. Slowly he went through the shack again, looking for anything else missing. As he expected, Francisco's favorite leather jacket was gone, as was his travel bag, his jeans, and his old cowboy boots. Francisco had not been torn from his bed. Francisco had packed carefully and deliberately, like someone who knows he's not coming back.

Ramon now understood the pattern in the chaos he had seen, but not been able to explain. The mess was too deliberate. It looked staged. The slit pillows served no purpose except to confuse the scene with a lot of loose feathers. No drugs or money had been hidden inside them. The important objects, like Diego's guitar, had been treated with respect and left in their place. Nobody had been looking for anything here. Francisco had created an artificial crime scene that appeared like a set in a CSI television show: the ransacked apartment, searched and torn apart, complete with slit pillows and overturned sofa.

"Nothing is what it seems at first," sighed Ramon.

Before he could be sure, he had to check one more detail. Ramon walked out of the shack and to the yard, where all the cars waiting to be repaired, as well as the junk cars Antonio used for spare parts, stood. As expected, Francisco's old blue Chevy Nova was not among them.

Slowly, Ramon walked back to the main house. His aunt and uncle still sat at the table, just as he had left them. Ramon joined them.

"Well," he began. "The good news is that Francisco is not dead."

His aunt and uncle looked up at him in surprise.

"What is the bad news?" his uncle Antonio asked.

"The bad news is that Francisco is not coming back," said Ramon.

Both hung their heads again. Ramon got up slowly and stroked his aunt's hair gently.

"Don't ever come back here," his uncle said quietly, before Ramon left the house.

52

SATURDAY, DECEMBER 28, 1:00 A.M.

Driving back north toward the border, Ramon replayed the events of December 18 in his mind. In light of what he had discovered at the shack, he needed to look at them from a different angle. Francisco had called him and said, "Diego is dead. I don't know what to do." Francisco's words suddenly took on a different meaning. Ramon had assumed that his cousin's cartel contacts had killed Diego. But Francisco had not actually said so, he had only implied it.

When Ramon had reached their meeting place, he had simply set in motion the plan to stage his own death. Francisco had been too agitated and confused to make any decisions. Ramon had attributed that to the shock over his brother's murder. Francisco had told him about Diego's refusal to smuggle drugs.

Now Ramon had to conclude that Francisco got rid of his brother, taking the entire drug commission, plus $10,000 from Ramon. Francisco was never in danger. He had done the cartel's job for them. Francisco intended to use Ramon as a witness to his innocence in Diego's murder, and it almost worked. He never anticipated Ramon's transformation of Diego's corpse into the artist himself.

The plan had bought Francisco more time. While Diego was officially "on vacation" in the Yucatán, he could relax. There was no connection between him and the dead Ramon. But once Ramon resurfaced and Francisco was faced with a rigorous police investigation, he chose to disappear.

Francisco wanted everybody to believe he had been kidnapped by the cartel. He had tried to cover his own tracks, and it almost worked. If it had not been for Rosa's picture . . .

Ramon drove north through the moonlit night under a clear and indifferent starry sky with one big question in his mind. Why had Francisco killed his brother? How had he been able to do something so horrible? Was he so terrified of the cartel? Was he afraid that if he did not kill Diego, the cartel would kill them both? Ramon had never known the kind of fear that must have driven his cousin to kill his own brother. Ramon was born in the United States and grew up in the knowledge that he was safe and free to do with his life what he wanted.

Ramon thought back to the many evenings he had spent with his cousins in the shack. His two cousins had been very different, just like he and Raoul were different. Diego was the sensitive, creative one. He loved music, his guitar; he was a dreamer, his mother's favorite. Ramon had to admit that Diego had also been his favorite of the two brothers. He felt an affinity with his artistic soul. Diego had helped him with projects like placing the wrapped stones in the desert as directional markers for the migrants, while Francisco had scoffed at the idea.

Diego had let his hair grow out like Ramon. Francisco was the practical one of the two. He thought art was a real waste of time and money. In his mind, placing rocks wrapped in red ribbon in the desert as Christmas gifts for the migrants was a fool's errand.

Ramon remembered an exchange between them one night, when Diego kept playing the ballad "Me and Bobby McGee" by Kris Kristofferson: "Freedom's just another word for nothing left to lose." Finally, Francisco couldn't take it anymore.

"Stop playing that stupid song," he'd snapped. "It's all nonsense."

"Why is it such nonsense?" Diego asked harmlessly.

"There is no freedom in having nothing. Having nothing means you are stuck in a shack. You can't do anything, you can't afford anything. You can't marry, you can't travel . . ."

Because Francisco had nothing, he hadn't been able to marry Rosa and save her life. Ramon heard the bitterness in his cousin's voice. Trying to ease the tension, he'd said, "Having a lot of possessions can also be a burden. You have to maintain them, you have to protect them; you have to pay taxes on them. You have to worry whether people like you for yourself or for what you own. I think that's what this song is trying to say."

"Easy for you to say," retorted Francisco angrily. "You have everything you want. You have a car, an apartment, a girlfriend, money, success . . ."

"Francisco, please," pleaded Diego. "Ramon worked for everything he has, and he gives away so much. He gives the gift of art."

"Diego, you are so naïve. You have nothing and you will never have anything; you can be sure of that."

"I have my guitar, I have my music, I have my family. I feel quite rich."

"You are such an idiot," Francisco's said angrily. Diego just kept strumming his guitar to the gentle tune.

Thinking about this exchange on the dark road north, Ramon felt a wave of grief and sadness wash over him. Diego had been such a kind soul. With painful clarity, he realized he would never hear Diego play his guitar again.

Ramon had to admit to himself that much of his conceptual art project staging his own death had really been about his own ego. It was about time to direct the attention away from himself and toward the memory of Diego. Diego, who did not deserve to die like that, just as no one deserved to die in that beautiful and horrible desert.

Francisco had resented Diego for his mild nature and easygoing manner that allowed him to be happy and content with what little he had. Francisco wanted more. He wanted to be respected. He wanted power and money. Was that enough reason to kill your own brother, if he got in the way? Ramon knew his brother Raoul was sometimes envious of him, but surely never enough to turn against him, or betray him. Was Francisco so driven by fear of the cartel and ambition that he had seen no other way?

Ramon approached the dozens of lanes of the San Ysidro border checkpoint. At this time of the night only a few cars idled in line, but the wait was still considerable. Over fifty million people crossed this border each year. Next to the waiting cars, beggars still held out their tin cans and a few tired salesmen attempted to peddle large teddy bears, Mexican blankets, coffee, and churros.

Ramon yawned. It had been a very long day. He had to make a difficult decision. Should he go back to the police and tell them that he believed his cousin had shot Diego, and that he based this conclusion on the missing picture of Francisco's high school sweetheart? Or should he just keep quiet? Diego was dead and Francisco was gone; what would he achieve by such a revelation?

Ramon had set in motion a complex sequence of events by staging his own death. He could not stop it now. He had to follow it to its end and see where it led.

When Ramon reached the Border Patrol agent in the small booth that separated Mexico from the US, the decision was made for him. The agent looked at his passport and checked his computer. He alerted a colleague and they waved Ramon over to secondary inspection. They did not return his ID. In the glaring lights of the fluorescent spotlight, they arrested Ramon and took him to a detention cell in handcuffs. It hadn't occurred to him until then that he was not supposed to leave the United States.

Sitting in the detention cell at the US–Mexican border, Ramon finally had time to slow down and reflect on his situation since his reemergence at his own funeral. He had a lot to process and to contemplate.

His motivation for faking his death had been simple: to bring awareness to the high cost of lives lost by migrants in the desert, and to
ensure that Diego was not just another statistic in that number. The
outcome was not so simple. He now knew that he had made some
major miscalculations.

Ramon looked around at the other prisoners in his cell. Several
ragged-looking Mexicans sat on the hard benches lining the walls.
Were they awaiting deportation to Mexico after being caught trying to
get into the US illegally? They eyed him suspiciously. He did not look
like them. His clothes were too nice and clean, his hair too long.

"Why are you here?" asked one of the men, dressed in dirty torn
jeans and thin tennis shoes. "You don't look like you belong here." His
hair was matted from dust and he had a bruise on his left cheek.

Ramon wanted to say, "I'm here because of you," but it sounded
arrogant and grandiose even to him. Instead he said, "Tell me why you
are here."

The man's eyes widened. "It's a long story," he said.

"I've got all night," Ramon answered.

The man told Ramon this had been his third attempt to reenter the
US. He had been arrested early in the morning by ICE officers and
brought here, away from his family, to be deported. He wanted to get
back to his job as a gardener and to his wife and two kids.

Another man told him that he had been stopped and arrested for
driving a car without a license. He hadn't done anything wrong, but
he'd been taken into custody and his fourteen-year-old-daughter, an
American citizen, was now on her own, without any parent.

A young inmate with curly hair, callused hands, and scared eyes
told Ramon he had been lost walking in the desert for three days
without water and food. His companion sprained his ankle and
couldn't go on. He'd barely made it out alive and feared the worst
about his friend.

Ramon asked if he'd ever seen any rocks wrapped in ribbons while
walking through the desert. The kid nodded. He said he'd followed
the rocks to a dirt road, but he wished they hadn't just been stones. The
rocks felt like a cruel joke to him. He needed water and food.

Ramon winced. His well-meaning art piece didn't stand up to the demands of the desert. Another miscalculation? At least his stones had led one man to safety.

Memories of Raoul and Diego emerged in his mind, as they had both helped him wrapping those stones with ribbons. They had worked near the Canyon Sin Nombre, where Diego died. Francisco had stayed home, claiming that he had more important things to do than wrap rocks. Nobody blamed him, but Diego and Raoul had worked alongside Ramon with concentration and focus. They didn't fully understand what Ramon was trying to do, but they respected him and his vision and loved him enough to spend their weekend doing this project with him. Together they distributed the rocks from Split Mountain Road through the elephant trees toward Highway 78 and safe passage. After all the rocks had been placed, like crumbs leading to safety, Diego, Raoul, and Ramon rested on boulders while Diego strummed his guitar. The desert glowed in the light of the setting sun as red as the small flowers on the ocotillo bushes. At this time of day, the desert felt peaceful.

"Why do you do what you do?" Raoul finally had asked his brother.

"Because it gives meaning to my life and to the world I live in," Ramon had answered.

"Does it give meaning to *my* life?" Raoul countered.

Ramon smiled. "It gives meaning to this afternoon and evening. You are here with Diego and me. We're sharing this moment. Isn't that meaningful in itself?"

Raoul pondered that. "Why do you play guitar, Diego?" he asked.

"It makes me happy," Diego answered, and he hummed a little tune by the Grateful Dead.

"I wish I had something that made me happy and gave me meaning," Raoul said.

"You have two sons and a wife, Raoul. That should give you plenty of meaning and happiness," Diego reminded him.

They all laughed, Raoul maybe a bit more awkwardly than the other two.

As the memory faded, Ramon was overcome with great affection for his brother and his cousin. Grief for Diego overwhelmed him, and he felt the loss deeply. A work of art in memory of his cousin began to take shape in his mind.

Ramon slipped out of his memory and back into the cell. "I'm sorry they were just rocks," he admitted. "I placed them there, as markers for a safe passage."

The men in the cell looked at him in astonishment. The kid with the smudged face and sad eyes said, "You did that? Maybe they helped to save my life, but they couldn't do anything for the friend I had to leave behind. I think about him every day—and every night," he added in a whisper.

The inadequacy of his installation hit Ramon like a slap in the face. Witnessing the pain of his cellmate helped him understand what his friends and family had felt when they believed him to be dead. He had been focused on his art but had failed to consider the devastating effect it would have on his family. Their love wasn't something to take lightly. It was a responsibility to take seriously.

Ramon had intended to honor Diego's memory by his deception, but instead he had provided cover for a murderer. A high cost. He had caused his mother great pain, something he had not really anticipated, figuring his absence was only temporary. But how could she know that? Now he regretted having put her through so much suffering. Hopefully his parents would forgive him—eventually.

What about his girlfriend Lizzie? Well, she wasn't his girlfriend anymore. He had left her when she was just about to forgive him. "If you leave now, don't bother coming back," she had said. He had made his choice. He had to accept the consequence. Lizzie was beautiful and fun, and she had made a real effort trying to find him, which he appreciated. But he hadn't really missed her on the beach of Akumal. If he was honest with himself, and this night seemed to be the time for honesty, he had to admit that art was his real mistress. He and Lizzie hadn't connected on a deeper level. Their attraction was mainly based on the fact that they "made such a pretty pair," the convenient pairing of an emerging artist and a gallery owner's daughter.

He had caused great suffering to his family, and for that he was heartbroken. Ramon never imagined that his brother could end up as a murder suspect. He had hoped that Raoul would step out of his shadow and realize his own strength. Maybe Raoul had emerged stronger, but not without a great deal of inner and outer turmoil, also causing a lot of pain for his family.

It was too late to stop the events he had set into motion in the Canyon Sin Nombre just ten days ago. He had to let them play out. There would be a trial. There would be headlines like "Conceptual Artist Arrested at Border Crossing." There would be a circus, as Lizzie had said. He had to ride it out. Ramon had meant to orchestrate a conceptual work of art by assuming Diego's identity. Now he realized that he, too, had been deceived. Francisco had double-crossed him, and he would stick to his original story. Leave Francisco out of it. Maybe one day he would reappear, either dead or alive.

He looked at the men in the cell. "Thank you for sharing your stories with me."

"What about you? What's your story? Why are you here?" the man with the bruise on his cheek asked.

"If you want to hear it, I'll tell you my story, full of misunderstandings and unintended consequences," Ramon said.

The prisoners nodded slowly.

"This better be good," one of them mumbled. "You don't have to be here; we have no choice."

53

SATURDAY, JANUARY 4, 1:00 P.M.

B ill stood at the counter of his Desert Rose Café looking out morosely over the empty dunes of the off-road desert park across the road from his trailer. A gentle breeze blew two tumbleweeds over the deserted parking lot and that was about it. Normally the week between Christmas and New Year was his busy time, with many holiday visitors. However, the double murder in the Canyon Sin Nombre, in contrast to the killing of the artist, had had a devastating effect. Tourists suddenly saw Borrego Springs as drug cartel territory where acts of great violence could happen at any time. The few who came avoided the area close to the Canyon Sin Nombre and the wind caves.

The door opened and brought in a gust of wind. Deputy Sheriff Thompson entered.

"Sheriff, what can I get you?" Bill asked.

"Just give me a beer."

Bill didn't strictly speaking have an alcohol license for his café, but who was going to report him? The sheriff of Borrego Springs?

After Thompson had taken a big swig from the beer bottle, he looked around the empty trailer.

"Business is pretty slow," he observed.

"Yeah, those two bodies your Deputy Ling found in the Canyon Sin Nombre haven't been good for the Desert Rose Café," Bill confirmed. He made it sound as if it were somehow Ling's fault.

"Tell me about it," Thompson sighed. "This mess just gets worse and worse."

"I hear the dead artist came back to life," Bill said.

"He has risen indeed."

Bill chuckled politely at the sheriff's joke. "Then who was the first dead body they found?" he asked.

"It was the artist's cousin, Diego Matus. He was a *pollero* and smuggled migrants across the border."

"So who killed the cousin?"

"Apparently the cartel contacts he met in the Canyon Sin Nombre, who picked up the migrants."

"Any particular reason?"

"Supposedly, the cousin refused to smuggle drugs."

"But I thought the brother identified the artist at the morgue?" Bill was still confused.

"Don't talk to me about the artist's brother, Raoul," Thompson responded bitterly. "Thanks to his false identification, the Borrego Springs Sheriff's Department is now being accused of shoddy police work. We should have taken fingerprints or DNA samples, they say. As if that would do any good if the victim had no record. Plus the case was crystal clear."

Bill shook his head. The case didn't seem very clear to him at all. "I know how you feel," he said thoughtfully. Bill, too, had once been falsely accused of running a sloppy operation for not adhering to strict food safety standards.

"It all seemed to make perfect sense," the sheriff continued. "Raoul identified the body, had a thing with the artist's girlfriend, then we thought he disappeared with the money across the border."

"Jeez, that sounds really complicated," considered Bill.

"Tell me about it. We had the artist's brother in custody when these two new bodies turned up, so we had to let him go."

"He couldn't have killed them?"

"No, he was already in jail."

Bill thought hard. "He still coulda killed the first guy, the cousin, or whatever you wanna call him."

"Couldn't have. Had an unbreakable alibi for that one."

Bill nodded gravely. "But why did the dead cousin wear the artist's clothes?" he asked.

"That's where it gets really messy. The artist dressed his dead cousin up in his clothes and put his ID into his pocket. 'A conceptual artwork,' he claims. He wanted to draw more attention to the high numbers of dead Mexicans in the desert," Thompson explained.

"Is that legal?" Bill was completely flabbergasted.

"Hell, no!" Sheriff Thompson still sounded outraged about the whole affair. "He's going on trial for tampering with evidence in a murder case and for misleading the authorities."

"Well, that's good, I suppose," Bill said.

"Not really," Thompson steamed. "The son of a bitch is planning to turn the trial into a circus about his 'conceptual artworks' and the cross-border issues, whatever that means."

"We do have a problem here—with the border, I mean," Bill agreed.

Thompson looked at him sharply and Bill immediately felt disloyal to his friend.

"I mean, it has gotten worse. We never had so many dead bodies before," he added.

This remark did not seem to comfort Thompson. "Give me another beer, Bill, will you?"

"Sure thing, Sheriff." Bill took another bottle of beer out of his fridge. "I'm sure you'll find the guys who did this," he added encouragingly.

"I don't think so, Bill," admitted Thompson. "The guys who killed the cousin are professional cartel hit men. There is nothing to link them to the murder and they are long gone on the other side of the border."

"But who were the two other bodies in the Canyon Sin Nombre?" Bill asked, still confused.

Thompson sighed. "Bill, we might never know who they were, but I think they were put there as a warning to us to back off. The cartel sent a message loud and clear: don't mess with this murder case, leave it alone, or else more people will die."

"Yeah, well. What are you gonna do?" Bill remarked philosophically.

They both sat in silence for a while, staring out over the empty dunes in the midday sun.

"I'm glad the holidays are over," Bill said finally.

"Me too. Always have been," Thompson agreed.

54

SUNDAY, JANUARY 5, 6:00 P.M.

Two hours northwest of Borrego Springs, the Ronald Cantor Gallery in Santa Monica was packed. Before being released on bail, Ramon had come up with a new installation in honor of Diego. This opening of his work at the Cantor Gallery doubled as a memorial celebration for his cousin.

The entire Matus family was there, the older Mr. Matus enthroned on a chair with Josefina beside him. Both sat very erect and didn't say a word.

Vega noticed Raoul stood behind his parents, close to Tina, who looked beautiful in a figure-hugging red dress. He looked self-confident and at ease with his arm around Tina's shoulder. Once in a while she looked at him with a radiant smile. The most dramatic change was his hair. Vega remembered his long hair from the "funeral" at the beach. He had cut it very short, and there was no more mistaking him for Ramon. What about their boys? Juan and Jaime sulked in a corner of the gallery, looking at the screens of their cell phones. Had their uncle's disappearance had an impact on them? Hard to tell, they were so absorbed in their game.

Had the Matus family forgiven Ramon, or were they just here to honor Diego? Vega wondered. With her sons she explored the installations, especially the new one, consisting of Diego's guitar, partially covered by a pile of sand. Ramon had installed a tape recorder inside, and through the sound hole Diego's voice from the telephone answering machine could be heard saying over and over again, "Hi. This is Diego. Are you there?" It also played several of Diego's songs, wistfully emerging from the sand.

Greg was talking to Ronald Cantor. Vega heard him negotiating the price for one of Ramon's flower drawings.

Jerome and Hilde Schlesinger stood with Ramon in the center of the gallery. Vega stole a glance at them once in a while to see how it was going. They seemed to be getting along.

"It's all about symbols," Jerome said.

"No," Ramon replied, "art is not about creating symbols that stand for something else. Art is about creating a new reality unlike the one the viewer lives in, but relatable."

"And delightful," added Jerome, accepting Ramon's correction.

Would Schlesinger and Ramon work together? Vega wondered. Why not? Both of them wanted to have an impact on people—Schlesinger by telling them how to think, Matus by getting them to look at and think about the world differently. Period. Ramon would approve of Schlesinger's Law #5: *Slow down the mind enough to hear your thoughts.* She had heard that Schlesinger's book was going into its second edition.

Even Detective Vincelli had made the trip up to Bergamot Station from San Diego. He was talking intently to Deputy Ling, who was looking sharp in a short, black dress.

". . . coming to San Diego," Vega overheard him say.

Was their conversation personal or professional in nature? Vega remembered seeing them together at the mock funeral for Ramon; maybe Ling was getting closer to her move to the San Diego Sheriff's Department.

Paula from *Los Angeles Magazine* took notes for an article about the exhibition.

The only people missing were Francisco and his parents. And Lizzie. Vega looked around, searching for her. Where was Lizzie? How could she not be at her own father's and boyfriend's exhibition opening? Unless it was over between her and Ramon. That was the only explanation. Lizzie had been so invested in finding out what happened to Ramon. Was she unable to forgive his deception? Apparently Ramon hadn't succeeded in regaining her trust. Vega couldn't blame her. Another victim of his "vision."

Vega recognized two museum curators, who inspected Ramon's installations closely, apparently more sympathetic to his vision. His profile in the art market had increased. A little notoriety always helped.

Vega's eye landed on the installation of a massive boulder casting a colorful shadow on the floor in a corner of the gallery. She remembered the meditation session on the first day of the winter solstice retreat and her dream of Ramon in the sunny Yucatán. She should have seen it. "What shadow did Ramon's death cast?" she had asked herself then. The ripple effect his disappearance had on his friends, his family, the art community, and the border region around Borrego Springs, the shadow his death cast, and the changes it triggered were Ramon's creation. It was right in front of her, but she had not seen it.

The death of Diego, believed to be Ramon, had cast a kaleidoscopic shadow. Vega wondered, had the incident with Ramon changed her? It had expanded her understanding of what a conceptual artwork could be. If some action had such a profound effect on so many lives, the art community, and even the Border Patrol, wasn't that worth something? Maybe even the definition of a masterpiece?

Obviously not for poor Francisco, who had been kidnapped . . . When she reached this point in her thoughts, Vega looked up and her eyes met Ramon's for a second. He gave her a quick ironic half-smile and then continued his conversation with Greg and one of the museum curators. *What's on your mind, Ramon?* Vega thought. *I will never truly understand it.* Greg came over and brought her a glass of wine.

"Congratulations, Vega," he said. "You are now the proud owner of a Ramon Matus flower drawing!"

"But . . ." Vega looked at him and thought about the ephemeral and conceptual nature of the flower installation, of the heaps of flowers on the beach in Coronado, and how the flowers were supposed to serve as a portal to the Yaqui world. She thought how all this definitely could not be captured in a drawing. Well, except as a souvenir, as a reminder to evoke this episode of the adventure in the Canyon Sin Nombre. The drawing would remind her of all the events, experiences, and their impact.

"What?" asked Greg.

"Nothing," she answered. "I love it that you bought the drawing." She smiled and remembered Spiritual Law #8: *Be in the moment. It will never come back and it's the only one you've got.* She raised her glass to Greg's and enjoyed the moment.

THE TEN LAWS OF MENTAL, EMOTIONAL, AND SPIRITUAL EXPANSION

BY JEROME SCHLESINGER

1. Act, don't react.
2. Believe and address the best in people and they will become so.
3. Don't avoid uncomfortable feelings and thoughts. Observe, investigate, and experience them fully.
4. Your body is 50 percent of your being. Don't neglect it, but don't overestimate it, either. Treat it well, but not too well.
5. Slow down the mind enough to hear your thoughts.
6. Forgive and let go—many times.
7. Don't compare yourself to others. Be happy with who you are!
8. Be in the moment. It will never come back and it's the only one you've got.
9. The more you think and do for others and forget about yourself, the happier you will be.
10. There are always more than two solutions to a problem—it's never "either/or," but rather "as well as." If a problem can't be solved, let it go. Give it to the cosmic washing machine.

ENDNOTES

All the characters in this novel are fictional, even though some were inspired by real people, dead or alive. The figure of Ramon Matus pays homage to the many talented, creative, smart, successful, and engaged Mexican-American artists who work in the border region.

La Casa Del Zorro was sold and closed down in 2007. It reopened under new ownership in 2013. Bertrand was inspired by Bernard, who died around the same time the original Casa Del Zorro closed. His former restaurant is now called Carmelita's and serves excellent Mexican food. The sign of the Desert Rose Café is still there, but the trailer that used to house it has been subdivided into three sections selling off-road vehicle paraphernalia and supplies.

The Border Patrol has been in the news constantly as they struggle with increasing numbers of migrants and refugees, and conflicting policies of what to do with them. According to sources inside the agency, the human and drug trafficking along the border is entirely controlled by the Mexican crime cartels. The migrants are victims of the cartels and the fluctuating immigration policies in the United States.

ACKNOWLEDGMENTS

It was fun to write this story and revisit some of my favorite places in the desert. I especially enjoyed coming up with Ramon's artworks and Jerome's spiritual laws.

I want to thank my husband Glen and sons Sebastian and Max, who always inspire me.

Thanks to my Sisters in Crime writing group, Valerie Hanson, Kim Keeline, Nicole Larson, Suzanne Haworth and Suzanne Shepard for giving me the feedback I needed and making this story much better.

My original critique group, Mary Kay Gardner and Edda Hodnett helped me with their encouragement and suggestions.

Thanks go to Lisa Wolff for her much needed copy-editing, and Scarlet Willette for the cover design.

I am grateful to Max and Sebastian Feye created earlier versions of the cover.

Dr. Carole Scott read an early version of the manuscript and provided valuable insights and corrections.

Thanks to the Border Angels for providing water, food and much needed aid to the migrants at the border.

Finally, I'm grateful for my readers who encourage me to keep on writing.

ABOUT THE AUTHOR

Cornelia Feye is an author, art historian and publisher. She published three mystery novels, and the first one, *Spring of Tears*, won the San Diego Book Award in 2011. The anthology *Magic Mystery & Murder*, co-edited with Tamara Merrill won the San Diego Book Awards in 2019. She is the founder of Konstellation Press, an indie publishing company for genre fiction and poetry. Her publications include art historical essays and reviews in English and German. www. konstellation-press.com

ALSO BY CORNELIA FEYE

Spring of Tears

San Diego Book Award Winner, 2011

Private Universe

Magic, Mystery & Murder

Short Story Anthology, San Diego Book Award Winner, 2018